Benziger Brothers

The new speller and word book

Benziger Brothers

The new speller and word book

ISBN/EAN: 9783741189074

Manufactured in Europe, USA, Canada, Australia, Japa

Cover: Foto ©Andreas Hilbeck / pixelio.de

Manufactured and distributed by brebook publishing software
(www.brebook.com)

Benziger Brothers

The new speller and word book

THE CATHOLIC NATIONAL SERIES.

THE

NEW SPELLER

AND

WORD BOOK

New York, Cincinnati, Chicago

BENZIGER BROTHERS

| PRINTERS TO THE | PUBLISHERS OF |
| HOLY APOSTOLIC SEE | BENZIGER'S MAGAZINE |

PREFACE.

This Speller has been prepared with the idea of making a pleasant task of a usually dry study, and, with this end in view, a variety of interesting exercises are given. As it is only by constant practice that the *habit* of correct spelling is formed, few rules will be found herein.

The lessons consist in part of

Familiar Words, such as enter into the home, church, and school life of every Catholic child.

Synonyms, a valuable intellectual training, which teach the nice distinctions in the meaning of words, and lead to the use of correct language in writing and speaking.

Homonyms, words pronounced alike, but spelled differ ently and with different meanings, ignorance of which is the source of many mistakes in spelling.

Words Commonly Mispronounced, or improperly accented.

Dictation Exercises, which show the proper words to be used.

Definitions, so that not only the orthography and pro- nunciation of the words are learned, but also their meaning.

Uncommon words and words rarely used find no place in this book. The usual matter found at the back of most Spellers, and seldom if ever used, is purposely omitted, and in its place practical Lessons are given to the very last page.

To insure absolutely correct pronunciation the words bear their **proper diacritical marks,** and these marks and the **syllabication** are strictly according to WEBSTER'S INTERNATIONAL DICTIONARY, the latest authority.

The fact that this Speller is **for the use of Catholic chil- dren exclusively** is never lost sight of, and many words are introduced which find no place in books intended for public schools.

The type, made expressly for this book, is large and clear, requiring no effort to read it, and the paper, printing, and binding are all that can be desired. It is hoped that this New Speller will meet the requirements of our Catholic Schools, and receive a warm welcome.

PHONIC MARKS USED IN THIS SPELLER.

VOWELS.

ā, long, as in dāy.

â, a modification of long ā, as in prefâce.

ă, short, as in făn.

â, as in bâre.

ä, with the Italian sound, as in cärt.

à, as in àsk.

ạ, broad, as in bạll.

ạ, obscure.

———

ē, long, as in bē.

ê, shorter than long ē, nearly like ĭ in ĭll, as in êvent.

ĕ, short, as in pĕn.

ē̃, before r, as in sē̃rve.

ẹ, obscure.

———

Ī, long, as in rīde.

ĭ, unaccented, as in ĭdea.

ĭ, short, as in sĭt.

ị, obscure.

———

ō, long, as in rōpe.

ô, unaccented, as in ôbey.

ŏ, short, as in chŏp.

ô, before r, as in hôrse.

ọ, obscure.

———

ū, long, as in blūe.

û, unaccented, a modification of long ū, as in ûnite.

ŭ, short, as in bŭt.

ụ, preceded by r, as in trụe.

û, before r, as in tûrn.

ụ, as in pụt.

———

o͞o, long, as in scho͞ol.

o͝o, short, as in lo͝ok.

ou, as in out.

oi, as in oil.

3

Table of Phonic Marks, continued.

ALPHABETIC EQUIVALENTS.

ạ, like short ŏ, as in whạt.

e̦, like long ā, as in obe̦y.

ê, before r, with the sound of â, as in thêre.

ew, like long ū, as in dew.

ee̦, like long ē, as in fēet.

ï, like long ē, as in pïque.

ï̦, before r, like ē, as in bïrd.

ȯ, like short ŭ, as in sȯn.

o̦, like long ōo, as in do̦.

ọ, like short ŏo, as in wọlf.

ow, like ou, as in owl.

oy, like oi, as in boy.

ȳ, like long I, as in flȳ.

y̆, like short ï, as in hy̆mn.

ỹ, like ē, as in mỹrrh.

CONSONANTS.

e, hard, like k, as in ꞓall.

ꞓ, soft, like s, as in ꞓivil.

ġ, soft, like j, as in larġe.

ꞩ, like z, as in haꞩ.

x̱, like gz, as in ex̱ample.

th, flat, as in with.

ṇ, like ng, as in uṇcle, iṇk.

THE NEW SPELLER

AND

WORD BOOK.

LESSON I.

of (ŏv)	our	now	bŭt
ăṣ	äre	dĭd	făt
one (wŭn)	lămp	pĕt	dāy

LESSON II. Written Exercise.

of   *are*   *pet*   *day*
one   *now*   *but*   *lamp*

LESSON III.

hĭṣ	ạll	ūṣe	yoŭ
bŏŏk	măn	sĕa	tĕll
whọ	Hĭm	sạw	bạll

LESSON IV. Written Exercise.

his   *man*   *use*   *you*
book   *all*   *sea*   *tell*
who   *Him*   *saw*   *ball*

LESSON V.

rōl*l*	hēa*r*	hâ*i*r	līk*e*
wĭl*l*	hōm*e*	côrd	down
hōp*e*	cōal	th*e*y	word (wûrd)
lŏv*e*	th̆ăt	wēr*e*	been (bĭn)

LESSON VI. Written Exercise.

roll   home   that   they
will   coal   were   like
love   down   been   cord
hope   hear   hair   word

LESSON VII.

Lôrd	dŏgs	th̆ĕn	rŭng
*h*our	hĕad	bĕl*l*	gŏŏd
mŭch	fĭrst	làst	whĕn (hwĕn)
th̆ĕm	màs*s*	mŭst	whạt (hwŏt)
rēad	sòm*e*	eām*e*	whīl*e* (hwīl)

LESSON VIII. Written Exercise.

dogs   first   much   read
some   last   when   what
good   hour   mass   must
then   rung   Lord   while

LESSON IX.

wĭth	yoûr	thêre	thĭnk
sōon	elăps	greăt	spēak
lĭve	thōṣe	hănds	thrēe

LESSON X. Written Exercise.

think　　*with*　　*soon*

your　　*claps*　　*hands*

great　　*live*　　*speak*

those　　*there*　　*three*

LESSON XI.

wĕnt	tōoth	elạwṣ	lĕarn
blăck	shärp	wạtch	săints
chĭld	mākes	trụth	priĕst
	twĕlve	chûrch	friĕnds

LESSON XII. Written Exercise.

truth　　*saints*　　*makes*

priest　　*watch*　　*twelve*

child　　*black*　　*sharp*

learn　　*church*　　*friends*

LESSON XIII.

knōw	eọuḷd	ŏn'lȳ	sēemed
taḷk	wạrm	eạḷḷed	laughs (läfs)
sīght	vĕr'ȳ	drēamed	brouǥht (bra̧t)

LESSON XIV. Written Exercise.

very   know   warm

sight   talk   called

only   could   seemed

laughs   brought   dreamed

LESSON XV.

waḷk	ăn'ġĕls	sĭs'tĕr	ŏth'ērs
hăve	bė fōre'	brŏth'ēr	a̧l'tar (-tĕr)
bā'bȳ	fä'thēr	lĭt'tle	pret' (prĭt'-) tȳ
	à bout'	mȯth'ēr	kĭt'ten

LESSON XVI. Written Exercise.

have   before   little

baby   father   kitten

about   mother   angels

altar   sister   pretty

LESSON XVII.

sĭl'vĕr	prâÿ'er	bûrn'ĭng	Sŭn'dåÿ
sĭm'ple	eăn'dles	flow'ērs	eŭn'nĭng
twĕn'tÿ	blĕss'ĕd	bow'ĭng	weâr'ĭng

LESSON XVIII. Written Exercise.

silver   bowing   blessed
simple   candles   Sunday
twenty   burning   cunning
prayer   flowers   wearing

LESSON XIX.

ĕv'ēr ÿ	prâiṣ'ĕṣ	eăn'nŏt
hĕav'en	plåÿ'fụl	mēan'ĭug
eȯv'ēred	pŭp'pleṣ	pĭe'tûres
vĕst'ment	sĭng'ĭng	ma'nÿ (mĕn'ÿ)
hănd'sȯme	swēet'ĕst	quĭ'ĕt (kwĭ'ĕt)

LESSON XX. Written Exercise.

every   praises   covered
playful   heaven   puppies
pictures   cannot   meaning
vestment   sweetest   handsome

REVIEW. LESSON XXI.

Short Sound of Vowels.

of	did	Him	with	have
fat	but	that	went	very
as	tell	dogs	rung	will
his	man	head	must	bell
book	lamp	twelve	much	them

Home is one of the sweetest words we know. When we hear the word home we think of those we love. We think of mother, father, sisters and brothers.

Tell us what you think of when you hear the word home.

REVIEW. LESSON XXII.

Long Sound of Vowels.

day	came	those	hope	coal
see	here	speak	soon	three
you	like	great	baby	only
roll	your	saints	know	quiet
read	child	use	home	sight
while	priest	they	tooth	makes

We have a little baby brother at home. He has only one tooth, and not much hair on his head. He cannot talk, but when we speak to him he laughs and claps his little hands. We all love him very much. I hope he will live to be a very good man.

REVIEW. LESSON XXIII.

Long Sound of Vowels.

praises	before	dreamed	meaning
angels	prayer	seemed	sweetest

Our baby has a pet kitten. It is as black as coal. It has sharp claws, but it is very playful. It will roll a ball of cord about and play with it for an hour. It is a pretty sight to watch the kitten while at play.

One day father brought home three cunning little dogs for brother, sister, and me. We called them Watch, Black, and Silver. They are so fat it makes us laugh to see them walk. The kitten did not like the little puppies at first, but now they are great friends, and will play all day. Our baby brother loves to watch the dogs and the kitten play.

REVIEW. LESSON XXIV.
Short Sound of Vowels.

pet	live	claps	hands
when	black	think	sister
been	little	Sunday	silver
then	pretty	blessed	kitten
good	simple	cannot	friends
many	heaven	vestments	twenty
every	candles	puppies	pictures

cunning   singing   handsome

I have a little friend who dreamed he was in heaven. This little child dreamed he saw our Lord, with the angels bowing down before Him and singing His praises. What a lovely dream that must have been! I hope we will all see our Lord in heaven one day, not in a dream, but in truth.

REVIEW. LESSON XXV.

Different Sounds of Vowels.

one	are	claws	father
all	what	watch	mother
who	Lord	church	others
love	there	warm	burning
Mass	first	brought	wearing
hair	some	about	covered

Last Sunday our church was lovely. The altar was covered with flowers. About twenty candles were burning, and there was a handsome silver lamp. The priest came in wearing a white vestment, and twelve boys went before him. When the little bell rung the church was so quiet it seemed like heaven.

REVIEW. LESSON XXVI.

our	ball	down	learn
now	word	walk	altar
saw	talk	truth	laughs
cord	hour	could	called
were	last	sharp	brother

I see you have a pretty prayer-book. It has many pictures: some of the Mass, and others of our Lord, His blessed mother, and the saints. The prayers are good, and so simple that a little child knows the meaning of every word. You must learn to read as soon as you can. Then you can use your book when you go to church.

LESSON XXVII.

fụll	whọm	shēep	ôr'chard (-chērd)
peâr	spĕnt	hôrs'ĕṣ	bōard'ĕd
eôrn	lămb	frụít	skĭp'pĭng
eowṣ	pēach	à-lŏng'	plĕaṣ'ant
nŭts	fïelds	ăp'ple	sŭm'mēr
tīme	wŏŏds	färm'ēr	eoŭn'trȳ

We had a very pleasant time in the country last summer. The farmer with whom we boarded had many horses, cows, and sheep.

It was a pretty sight to see a little lamb skipping by the side of its mother.

We spent our days in the fields, the orchard, and the woods. There were fields of corn and orchards full of sweet fruit. There were apple trees, pear trees, and peach trees in the orchard. In the woods were trees covered with nuts.

LESSON XXVIII. Words often Misused.

(Fill out the blanks with the right words.)

I
me
Who took the basket to my aunt? — did.
Did you not see —?

to
at
Were you — home to-day?   No; I went
— church.

like
love
I — my brother and sister. I — apples and
pears.

can
may
Mother, — I go out to play? Not to-day;
you — go to-morrow.

her
she
Who was laughing in church this morning?
— was. I saw —.

lay
lie
I think I shall — down a while.   — that book
on the table.

learn
teach
My aunt promises to — me French. I think I
can — it very soon.

set
sit
Mary — that lamp on the table, and then –
down by me.

stop
stay
How long did you — in the country? The
train does not — here.

let
leave
— me alone. I am busy now. — me. I wish
to be alone.

LESSON XXIX. Vegetables.

bēets	tûr'nĭps	ăs pär'à gŭs	lĕt'tuçe (-tĭs)
çĕl'ēr y̆	eăb'bȧ̇ge	spĭn'ȧch (-ȧj)	eau̯'lĭ flow'ēr
pärs'le y̆	pô tä'tôe̤ş	pärs'nĭp	ȯn'ion (-y̆ŭn)
eăr'rȯts	tȯ mä'tôe̤ş	pŭmp'kĭn	squȧsh (skwŏsh)

LESSON XXX. Fruits.

peâr	pēach	chĕr'ry̆	eăn'tȧ lọupe
plŭm	lĕm'ȯn	eŭr'rant	pĭne'-ăp'ple
grāpe	çĭt'rȯn	ä'prĭ eŏt	ŏr'ange (-ĕnj)
ăp'ple	mĕl'ȯn	bȧ nä'nȧ	quĭnçe (kwĭns)

LESSON XXXI. Trees.

ăsh	bĭrch	ạl'dĕr	lĭn'den
yew	bēech	çē'dar (-dĕr)	wĭl'lȯw
ōak	lärch	mä'ple	wạl'nŭt
gŭm	sprụçe	pŏp'lar (lēr)	hĭck'ȯ ry̆
pĭne	hä'zel	lō'eŭst	sy̆e'ȧ mōre

LESSON XXXII. Parts of a Tree.

săp	bou_gh_	trŭṉk	lēa_ves_
rōot	bärk	ve_i_ns	brȧnch'ĕ̤ş
bŭds	fru_i_t	lĭm_b_s	blŏs'sȯms

LESSON XXXIII. Birds.

_w_rĕn	thrŭsh	ō'rĭ ōle	pär'trĭ_d_ge
fĭnch	rŏb'ĭn	· spär'rȯ_w_	bŏb'ȯ lĭṉk
erȯ_w_	grouse	swạl'lȯ_w_	hŭm'mĭng bĭrd

LESSON XXXIV.

fĭne	tŏŏk	spāde	bâs'kĕt
pṵt	sănd	found	găth'ēred
dŭg	mīles	tīred	wĕath'ĕr
out	äᵤnt	thrō𝑤n	rēached
fĭsh	whīle (hwĭl)	á wāy'	sēa' shōre
	fīve	Mȧ'rў	shĕlls

One day while we were in the country our aunt Mary took us to the sea-shore, which is five miles away. It was fine weather and sister and I played about on the sand. She gathered some pretty shells, which she found on the sand, and put them into a basket: I dug up the sand with my little spade, and I found a fish that had been thrown upon the shore. We had a good time, but were tired out when we reached home.

LESSON XXXV. Names of Colors.

rĕd	ŏl'ĭve	ĭn'dĭ gô	ŏr'anġe (ĕnj)
pĭnk	ăm'bēr	sẵl'm'ön	ĕm'ēr a̯ld
blūe	lĕm'ŏn	vī'ô lĕt	grȧss' grēen
lĭ'la̯e	yĕl'lŏw	seär'lĕt	bŏt'tle grēen
grēen	pûr' ple	erĭm'şon	vēr mĭl'ion (-yŭn)

LESSON XXXVI.

eŏld	sŏft	wrăp	drĕss'ĕş
yärn	whĭch	elŏth	wĭn'tēr
dȳed	eŏats	kĭnds	wŏŏl'ĕn
vĕsts	grŏws	ought (a̯t)	eŏt'ton
gĭrls	elŏaks	eŏl'ors (-ērs)	chēap'ēr

LESSON XXXVII.

mȧde	clŏth'ĭng	vä'rĭ o̯ŭs	ăn'ĭ ma̯ls
eẵtch	trou'şērş	elēaned	mȧ tē'rĭ a̯l
wŏv'en	eûrled	wa̯rm'ĕst	our sĕlveş'

When we go out in winter we ought to wrap ourselves up so as not to catch cold; then we can stay out all day.

Woolen clothing is the warmest. Boys wear coats, vests, and trousers of wool. Girls have cloaks and dresses of the same material.

Wool is the soft, curled hair which grows on sheep and other animals. It is cut off, cleaned, and made into yarn. This is dyed of various colors, and then woven into cloth. Some cloth is made of wool and cotton, and cheaper kinds of cotton only.

LESSON XXXVIII. Clothing.

eăp	shọe	hōṣe	ȧ'pron (-pŭrn)
mŭff	shïrt	eðat	mĭt'tĕn
hăt	skïrt	bŏn' nĕt	nĕck'tĭe
eŭff	gown	jăck'ĕt	eŏl'lar (-lẽr)
bōͦt	glóve	gȧi'tẽrs	wrăp'pẽr
sŏck	shạwl	erȧ văt'	stŏck'ĭng

LESSON XXXIX.

Write a list of words that have the following sounds:

ā, as in dā*y*;	à, as in là*s*t;	ĕ, as in tĕll;
â, as in sĕn'âte;	ạ, as in ạl'tar;	ê, as in thêre;
ă, as in făt;	ạ, as in whạt;	ẹ, as in thẹy;
â, as in hâ*i*r;	ð, as in hē*a*r;	ē, as in lē*a*rn;
ä, as in fä'thẽr;	ḙ, as in ḙ vĕnt';	I, as in lĭk*e*;

LESSON XL.

Write another list of words that have the following sounds:

ĭ, as in hĭ*ṣ*;	ọ, as in *w*họ;	ū, as in ū*ṣe*;
ï, as in fïrst;	ọ, as in cọ*ul*d;	ŭ, as in bŭt;
ō, as in hōm*e*;	ô, as in côrd;	ụ, as in trụth;
ŏ, as in dŏg;	oͦo, as in boͦot;	ụ, as in fụll;
ọ, as in lóve;	ŏͦo, as in gŏͦod;	û, as in chûrch;

LESSON XLI. Names of Animals.

hĕn	cä*l*f	snāk*e*	tī'gẽr	bēa'vẽr
hŏg	erōw	hound	eăm'ĕl	chĭck'ĕn
dŭck	mūle	wọlf	tûr'keў	mŏn'keў
hâre	quai*l*	pō'nў	răb bĭt	eȧ nā'rў
hôrse	goͦose	li'ón	gŏṣ'lĭng	ĕl'ḙ phant

LESSON XLII. Human Sounds.

cry̆	sīgh	snōre	shout
yĕll	lĭsp	bawl	whoop
hŭm	rănt	yawn	spēak
talk	gāpe	grōan	shriēk
sĭng	mōan	snärl	screām

LESSON XLIII. More Human Sounds.

tĭt′tẽr	stŭt′tẽr	cough (kaf)
gĭg′gle	prăt′tle	laugh (läf)
mŭt′tẽr	hăl loo′	whĭs′pẽr (hwĭs′pẽr)
mûr′mŭr	snēeze	whĭs′tle (hwis′l)
sĭm′pẽr	stăm′mẽr	hĭc′cough (-kŭp)

LESSON XLIV. Kinds of Motion.

rāçe	crawl	glīde	waltz (walts)
lĭmp	clīmb	trămp	cā′pẽr
walk	dànçe	märch	bounçe
crēep	slīde	prànçe	trŭdge

LESSON XLV. Other Kinds of Motion.

tŏt′tẽr	trăv′ĕl	säun′tẽr	stăg′gẽr
căn′tẽr	tŏd′dle	scăm′pẽr	stŭm′ble
ăm′ble	tŭm′ble	clăm′bẽr	străg′gle
găl′lŏp	hŏb′ble	shŭf′fle	scrăm′ble

LESSON XLVI. Family Relations.

sȯn	ŭn′cle	coŭş′in	kĭn′drĕd
wīfe	pâr′ent	wĭd′ōw	chĭl′drĕn
äunt	fä′thẽr	nĕph′ew (nĕf′ū)	rĕl′à tĭve
nīēçe	mȯth′ẽr	hŭş′band	wĭd′ōw ẽr
sĭs′tẽr	brȯth′ẽr	făm′ĭ ly̆	daugh′tẽr

LESSON XLVII. Words often Misused.

(Fill out the blanks with the right words.)

saw seen	I have not — your sister since she returned home, but I — your brother yesterday.
gone went	Father Smith has — out of town. He called on me the day before he — away.
best better	Of the two horses, I think the gray one is the —; in fact, it is one of the — I have ever seen.
except unless	— it should rain, all our party will go to the Fair — my brother, who is sick.
were was	I have heard that the last Fair — the most successful ever held. There — many people there.
expected supposed	Every one is — to know that he is — to be quiet and orderly in church.
good well	That lawyer speaks —. He has a — voice.
who whom	— do you suppose I met yesterday? A man — went to school with me when I was a boy.
is are	That marigold · ~ a pretty flower, but these violets — sweeter.
round around	The shelves are — the room. The sailor made a voyage — the world.

LESSON XLVIII. Parts of a House.

brĭck	wạl*l*s	dōors	lĕ*a*d′ĕr
stŏn*e*	môr′tar (-tēr)	wĭn′dŏ*w*s	glàs*s*
wŏŏd	çê mĕnt′	rōoms	lŏcks
bĕ*a*ms	stâ*i*rs	çĕl′lar (lĕr)	çĕĭl′ĭng
rōŏf	flŏors	gŭt′tēr	băl′ŭs tērs

LESSON XLIX. Kinds of Buildings.

vĭl′là	păl′âçe	mŏsq*ue*	băr′r*a*ck
eăb′ĭn	chăp′ĕl	sў̆n′à gŏg*ue*	ja*i*l
eŏt′tȧg*e*	chûrch	stŏr*e*	prĭ§′on
shăn′tў̆	tĕm′pl*e*	fă*e*′tŏ rў̆	th§′à tēr
eăs′*t*le	eȧ thĕ′dr*a*l	wâre′hous*e*	hŏ tĕl′

LESSON L. Names of Carpenters' Tools.

fĭl*e*	drĭl*l*	squâre	eŏm′pas*s*
vĭs*e*	lĕv′ĕl	plῐ′ĕr§	eăl′ĭ pēr§
brâçe	chĭ§′ĕl	gĭm′lĕt	serew′drĭv′ĕr
plăn*e*	ạ*u*′gēr	rĕam′ĕr	mῐ′tēr bŏx

LESSON LI. Names of Occupations.

brŏ′kẽr	grŏ′çẽr	tā*i*′lor (-lẽr)	ärt′ĭst
hăt′tẽr	bă ̣nk′ẽr	prĭnt′ẽr	flŏ′rĭst
mĭl*l*′ẽr	eŏŏp′ẽr	bu*t*ch′ẽr	tûrn′ẽr
ă*c*et′or (-ẽr)	sâ*i*l′or (-ẽr)	pā*i*nt′ẽr	ĕn grāv′ẽr
sŏl′dier (-jẽr)	lạ*w*′yẽr	bu*i*ld′ẽr	pŭb′lĭsh ẽr

LESSON LII. Out-of-door Sports.

tĕn′ nĭs	bō*w*l′ ĭng	e-rĭck′ ĕt	sle*igh*′ ĭng
rĭd′ ĭng	skăt′ ĭng	bōat′ ĭng	e-rŏ qu*ȩt*′ (-kȧ′)
rō*w*′ ĭng	fĭsh′ ĭng	bāth′ ĭng	rŭn′nĭng
sâ*i*l′ ĭng	drĭv′ ĭng	swĭm′mĭng	jŭmp′ ĭng
nŭt′ tĭng	lĕap′ ĭng	shōōt′ ĭng	bâse′ bạl*l*

LESSON LIII.   Articles found in a Kitchen.

mŏp	bā'sĭn	tŭm'blēr	sĭde′ bōard′
sōap	bȧs'kĕt	pĭtch'ēr	tŏw'ĕl (tou'ĕl)
tŏngs	dĭp'pēr	dŭst'păn	dĕm' ĭ jŏhn
erṇ'ĕt	pĭp'kĭn	eăd'dў	flăt′ ĭ'ron (ĭ'ŭrn)
erŏck	hăm'pēr	dĭsh'elŏth'	ănd′ ĭ' ron (-ĭ'ŭrn)
săl'vēr	eăn' ĭs tēr	kĭn'dlĭngs	grĭd′ĭ'ron (-ĭ'ŭrn)

LESSON LIV.   Articles in the Pantry.

jär	eȧst' ēr	strāin' ēr	knĭfe′ bōard′
jŭg	tū rēen′	tĭn' wâre	skew' ēr (skū'ēr)
chĕst	năp' kĭn	tēa 'ûrn	chăf' ĭng dĭsh′
trāy	erŏck' ēr ў	eŏl′ an dēr	nŭt′ erăck′ēr
flȧsk	spĭç' ĕṣ	vĭct' uals	sạlt′ çĕl lar (-lēr)

LESSON LV.   Occupations.

eŏŏk	wāit′ ēr	sāleṣ' man	bŏŏk′ kēep ēr
clērk	fŏŏt′ man	gŏv′ ērn ĕss	bŏd′ ў sērv ant
bŭt′ lēr	eŏach' man	tū' tor (-tēr)	la′ dў'ṣ māid′

LESSON LVI.   Parts of the Body.

tōe	jaw	shĭn	nōṣe	eălf
hĭp	nāil	fĭst	fāçe	lĭmb
ĕar	sōle	chĭn	hĕad	thĭgh
ärm	fŏŏt	nĕck	hănd	wrĭst
lĕg	hēel	lĭps	knēe	thŭmb

LESSON LVII.   Other Parts of the Body

chĕst	tēeth	tŏngue	lăsh′ ĕṣ
wāist	pälm	tĕm' ple	eye'brow (ĭ'brou)
loins	thrōat	ăṇ' kle	fŏre′ hĕad
chēek	brĕast	ĭn' stĕp	shŏul′ dēr
mouth	knŭe'kle	fĭṇ' gēr	ĕl' bŏw

REVIEW. LESSON LVIII.
Long sound of ā.

may	face	lay	hazel
stay	plane	brace	maple
race	grape	basin	canary
tray	spade	caper	various
made	Mary	apron	potatoes
snake	away	apricot	tomatoes

REVIEW. LESSON LIX.
Long sound of ā represented by ā, ai, and e̤.

jail	veins	gaiters	chafing-dish
they	quail	tailor	engraver
waist	waiter	strainer	salesman
stain	sailor	painter	lady's maid

REVIEW. LESSON LX.
Short sound of ă.

rant	actor	canter	stammer
hand	travel	tramp	scamper
prattle	amble	gallop	balusters
catch	hatter	clamber	asparagus
chapel	napkin	barrack	cantaloupe

REVIEW. LESSON LXI.
Short sound of ă.

caddy	castle	lamb	stagger
salver	banker	apple	cravat
hamper	ankle	carrots	canister
cabin	lashes	factory	flat-iron
jacket	amber	calipers	wrapper
camel	palace	salmon	scramble
rabbit	family	cabbage	andiron
shanty	sparrow	gathered	animals

REVIEW. LESSON LXII.

Sound of â and ê, like â in *air ;* a̦ and ô, like a̦ in *all.*

hare	jaw	hair	parent
corn	pear	horse	orchard
walk	shawl	talk	daughter
there	cord	cough	warehouse
yawn	altar	waltz	salt-cellar
crawl	auger	square	cauliflower

REVIEW. LESSON LXIII.

Sound of ä, as in *arm,* and of ȧ, as in *ask.*

last	jar	bark	laugh
calf	gape	flask	palm
glass	yarn	larch	march
snarl	aunt	dance	basket

REVIEW. LESSON LXIV.

Sound of ä, as in *arm,* and of ȧ, as in *ask,* continued.

caster	farmer	banana
artist	scarlet	parsnips
father	branches	partridge
saunter	parsley	grass-green

REVIEW. LESSON LXV.

Sound of long ē, as in *tea.*

ear	beets	sheep	shriek
heel	trees	creep	sneeze
knee	speak	niece	scream
cheek	hear	green	cedar
teeth	beech	peach	leaves

REVIEW. LESSON LXVI.
Long sound of ē, as in *tea*, continued.

fields	beaver	leaders	cleaned
beams	reamer	ceiling	reached
theater	material	tureen	cathedral

REVIEW. LESSON LXVII.
Sound of ē and of ī, like ē in *ermine*.

were	shirt	birch	skirt
first	learn	girls	clerk

REVIEW. LESSON LXVIII.
Short sound of ĕ, as in *tell*.

went	head	vests	lemons
yell	neck	hotel	pleasant
wren	chest	breast	elephant
best	shells	lettuce	ourselves

REVIEW. LESSON LXIX.
Short sound of ĕ, continued.

spent	better	cellar	emerald
level	cement	temple	relative
elbow	melons	dresses	necktie
cherry	celery	nephew	expected
except	yellow	weather	demijohn

REVIEW. LESSON LXX.
Long sound of ī, as in *time*.

fine	like	tired	miles
file	five	while	violet
vise	slide	pliers	miterbox
wife	thigh	climb	sideboard
lion	lilac	glide	knifeboard
sigh	tiger	kinds	pineapple

REVIEW. LESSON LXXI.

Short sound of Ĭ, as in *is*.

his	lips	chin	wrist
sit	fish	brick	villa
hip	sing	limb	linden
fist	lisp	finch	mitten
shin	pink	limp	quince

REVIEW. LESSON LXXII.

Short sound of Ĭ, continued.

drill	titter	miller	chicken
dipper	which	prison	sister
pipkin	chisel	gimlet	builder
widow	winter	printer	crimson
giggle	whistle	willow	simper

REVIEW. LESSON LXXIII.

Short sound of Ĭ, concluded.

citron	windows	victuals	widower
finger	kindred	pitcher	gridiron
instep	children	hickory	kindlings
spinach	hiccough	tinware	dishcloth
indigo	whisper	skipping	vermilion

REVIEW. LESSON LXXIV.

Long sound of ō, as in *toe*.

cold	oak	crow	doors
hose	pony	nose	moan
sole	floors	soap	oriole

soldier   boarded   coachman

REVIEW. LESSON LXXV.

Long sound of ō, continued.

store	snore	grows	grocer
coats	broker	thrown	florist
groan	stone	locust	clothing
throat	cloaks	woven	shoulder

REVIEW. LESSON LXXVI.

Short sound of ŏ, as in *dog*.

hog	soft	gone	totter
mop	olive	along	mosque
sock	crock	poplar	hobble
cloth	robin	cotton	collar

REVIEW. LESSON LXXVII.

Short sound of ŏ, as in *dog*, and ạ, as in *what*.

locks	oranges	squash	crockery
toddle	gosling	blossoms	bobolink
bonnet	cottage	forehead	bottlegreen
swallow	stocking	walnut	body servant

REVIEW. LESSON LXXVIII.

Sound of ōō, as in *boot;* ọ, as in *who;* and ô before r.

shoe	whom	halloo	whoop
root	goose	mortar	rooms

REVIEW. LESSON LXXIX.

Sound of ŏŏ, as in *foot;* also represented by ọ and ṳ.

took	put	cook	cooper
woods	wolf	could	footman
butcher	full	woolen	bookkeeper

REVIEW. LESSON LXXX.

Long sound of û, as in *blue*, and represented by ew, as in
yew; also the sound of u, when preceded by *r*,
and of û, as in *burn.*

glue	cruet	church	turner
mule	fruit	turkey	skewer
truth	spruce	purple	turnips
tutor	curled	murmur	screwdriver

REVIEW. LESSON LXXXI.

Short sound of ŭ, as in *but;* and represented by ŏ, as in *love.*

son	duck	onion	jumping
dug	buds	currant	shuffle
plum	trunk	summer	mother
cuff	uncle	country	husband
glove	colors	thrush	tumbler

REVIEW. LESSON LXXXII.
Short sound of ŭ, continued.

muff	mutter	brother	stutter
gutter	trudge	stumble	publisher
thumb	monkey	pumpkin	compass
tongue	tumble	dustpan	nutcracker
cousin	colander	governess	humming bird

REVIEW. LESSON LXXXIII.
Unmarked Letters.

out	ought	shout	found
gown	loins	hound	grouse
cows	bough	mouth	bounce

REVIEW. LESSON LXXXIV.
Long and short sound of y.

cry	dyed	eyebrow
sycamore		synagogue

LESSON LXXXV. In the Schoolroom.

dĕsk	cha̱lk	lĕt' tērs	point' ēr
bĕnch	spónġe	erāy' ón	seẖŏl' ar (-ĕr)
slāt*es*	chärts	pĕn' çĭl	tēach' ēr
bŏŏks	ru̱l' ēr	stū' dent	ĭn̠k' wĕl*l*s
măps	pū' pĭl	nŭm' bĕrs	blăck' bōard
glōb*e*	fĭg' ûr*es*	rŭb' bĕrs	mŏn' ĭ tor (-tēr)

LESSON LXXXVI. In a Kitchen.

dĭsh	rānġe	boil' ēr	sa̱uçe' păn
pai̱l	brŭsh	bŭck' ĕt	seŭt' tle
bōwl .	la̱' dle	grāt' ēr	skĭl' lĕt
óv' *en*	brŏŏm	tōast' ēr	broil' ēr
stōv*e*	pōk' ēr	kĕt' tle	skĭm' mēr
sĭev*e*	shóv' *el*	grĭd' dle	sōap' dĭsh'

LESSON LXXXVII. Articles of Food.

bŭns	mŭf' fĭns	mó lås' se̱ş	bēef' steāk
fĭsh	bĕr' rĭe̱ş	eătch' ŭp	whēat eāk*es*
ĕg*g*s	săl' *a*d	sa̱u' såġ eş	dōu*gh*' nŭts
hòn' eў	pĭck' l*es*	flăp' jăcks	ăp' ple frĭt' tērs
eŏf' fê*e*	bĭs' *eu*ĭt	prê şērv*es*'	măe' à rō' nĭ

su̱g' ar (shŏŏg' ēr)   chow' (chou'-) dēr

LESSON LXXXVIII. Things about our Rooms.

vās*e*	lounġe	pĭ àn' ô	rŏck' ēr
rŭgs	sō' fà	eär' pĕt	măt' trĕs*s*
lămp	tā' b*l*e	măt' tĭng	bĕd' stĕ*a*d
châi̱r	bōl' stēr	*e*rā' dle	eûr' tai̱ns
elŏck	oil' *e*lōth	pĭl' lō*w*	wa̱rd' rōb*e*

bŏŏk' *e*ās*e*   quilt (kwĭlt)   bū' reau. (-rô)

wa̱sh' stănd   găs' fĭx' tûr*e*   wĭn' dō*w* shād*e*

LESSON LXXXIX. More Tools.

fŏrġe	wrĕnch	clĕav′ẽr	trow′ĕl (trou′ĕl)
ăn′vĭl	măl′lĕt	bĕe′tle	hăm′mẽr
gauġe	nĭp′pẽrṣ	pĭn′çẽrṣ	plŭmb′lĭne
rĕam′ ẽr	hăṭch′ĕt	crŏw′bär′	grĭnd′stŏne

LESSON XC. Colors and Shades of Color.

grāy	hă′ zĕl	çĭt′ rĭne	mȧ ġĕn′ tȧ
bŭff	sŏr′ rĕl	eär′ mĭne	whĭte (hwĭt)
drăb	rŭs′ sĕt	lăv′ ĕn dẽr	brown (broun)
blăck	mȧ rōŏn′	ạu′ bûrn	mauve (mōv)
rụ′ bў	elăr′ ĕt	chĕsṭ′ nŭt	ăz′ ure (ăzh′ ụr)

LESSON XCI. Animals.

gŏat	hĕïf′ ẽr	wĕa′ ṣel	wŏŏd′chŭck′
ŏx′ en	sĕt′ tẽr	ẽr′ mĭne	spăn′ iel (-yĕl)
lўṇx	point′ ẽr	tẽr′ rĭ ẽr	pôr′ eû pĭne
beâr	jăck′ ạl	răe cōŏn′	guĭn′ êa pĭg′

LESSON XCII. More Animals.

shĕep	mär′ tĕn	reịn′ dĕer	erŏ′ eȯ dĭle
mĭṇk	dŏṇ′ keў	ăn′ tê lōpe	lĕop′ ard (-ẽrd)
mōŏse	mȧs′ tĭff	hў ê′ nȧ	ăl′ lĭ gā′ tor (-tẽr)
zē′ brȧ	păn′ thẽr	bŭf′ fȧ lō	squir′ rel (skwẽr′rĕl)

LESSON XCIII. More Food.

rŏll	flour	grā′ vў	pŏr′ rĭdġe
mĕal	brĕad	eȯ′ eȯa	păn′ eăke
mŭsh	sạuçe	erŭl′ lẽr	swĕet′ mĕat
brŏth	jĕl′ lў	erăck′ ẽr	chŏe′ ȯ lăte
dŏugh	grụ′ ĕl	dŭmp′ lĭng	eŭs′ tard (-tẽrd)
pĭe	wạf′ fle	sănd′ wĭch	mär′ mȧ lăde

LESSON XCIV. Vegetables.

ŏats	rȳe	gär' lïe	răd' ĭsh ĕş
pĕaş	flăx	bär' leў	mŭsh' rōoms
rïçe	bēanş	erĕss' ĕş	eū' cŭm bẽrş
eôrn	mа̄ize	rhụ' bärb	wheat (hwēt)

LESSON XCV. Animal Food.

hăm	gāme	eŭt' lĕt	vĕn' ĭ şon
loin	lămb	oys' tẽr	sălm' ȯn
pŏrk	elăm	răsh' ẽr	mŭs' cles
chŏp	trïpe	tûr' keў	fowl (foul)

LESSON XCVI. Tools.

hōe	lĕ' vẽr	pïck	bĕv' el
ạwl	lăthe	pŭnch	slĕdġe
ădz	răke	scȳthe	shēarş
sạw	rïv' ĕt	spāde	shȯv' el

LESSON XCVII. Studies,

spĕll' ĭng	mū' şĭe	wẹights	à rïth' mê tïe
rēad' ĭng	hĭs' tô rȳ	mĕaş' ûres	eŏm' pŏ şï' tion
writ' ĭng	bŏt' à nȳ	dïe tă' tion	ġê ŏg' rà phȳ
drạw' ĭng	ăl' ġê brà	lăṉ' guâġe	eăt' ê ehĭşm

LESSON XCVIII. The Months and their Abbreviations.

Jăn' û à rȳ	Jăn.	Jû lȳ'	Jùl.
Fĕb' rụ à rȳ	Fĕb.	Ạu' gŭst	Ạug.
März	Mär	Sĕp tĕm' bẽr	Sept.
Ā' prĭl	Āpr.	Ŏe tô' bẽr	Oet.
May	May	Nȯ vĕm' bẽr·	Nȯv.
Jūne	Jūne	Dê çĕm' bẽr	Dêç.

LESSON XCIX. Articles of Food.

bĕef	lĭv′ ēr	vēal	pṳd′ dĭng
sọṵp	erēam	hăsh	ŏm′ ê lĕt
chēeᶊe	bŭt′ tēr	stew	frĭe′ *as* sēe′
mĭlk	mŭt′ ton	pās′ trȳ	swēet′ brĕad

LESSON C. Covering for Hands and Feet.

hōᶊe	elȫg	mĭt′ tĕn	stŏck′ ĭng
sŏck	pŭmp	păt′ tĕn	gȧ lŏᶜhe′
bŏŏt	mŭf*f*	slĭp′ pēr	mŏe′ eạ sĭn
shọe	glòve	săn′ dạl	gäṵnt′ lĕt

LESSON CI. Metals and Minerals.

tĭṉ	brȧss	spĕl′ tēr	ĭ′ ron (ĭ′ ṵrn)
zĭṉe	stēel	nĭck′ *el*	mēr′ eṵ rȳ
gōld	eŏp′ pēr	eō′ bạlt	plŭm bā′ gȯ
lĕad	sĭl′ vēr	ġȳp′ sŭm	pew′ tēr (pṳ′ ter)

LESSON CII. Other Minerals.

flĭnt	jăs′ pēr	erȳs′ tạl	sōap′ stōne′
slāte	pĕb′ ble	sănd′ stōne′	brown′ stōne′
ȯ′ nȳx	mär′ ble	blūe′ stōne′	ăd′ ȧ mȧnt
ăg′ ȧte	grăn′ ĭte	lĭme′ stōne′	quạrtz (kwạrts)

LESSON CIII. Terms used in Mechanics.

eăm	erănk	jĭm′mȳ	erōɯ′ bär′
gēar	pĕd′ ạl	tăe′ *k*le	hănd′ spĭke
wĭnch	ăx′ le	trĕad′le	wheel (hwĕl)
lĕ′ vēr	pṳl′ leȳ	wĕd*g*e	serew (skrṵ)
shȧft	eăp′ stăn	ĕn′ ġĭne	pĭn′ ion (-yŭn)

LESSON CIV. Words relating to Sewing.

fĕll	därn	eŏt' ton	trăns' fẽr
pătch	băste	nēe' dle	hĕm' stĭtch
mĕnd	wĕlt	shēarş	băck' stĭtch
yōke	sēam	gŭs' sĕt	ĕm' ēr ў băg
sĭlk	thrĕad	bŏd' kĭn	ĕm broid' ēr
bănd	ĭn sẽrt'	thĭm' ble	scĭş' şorş (-zẽrz)
ŏ' pen work (wûrk)		tāpe' meas ûre (-mĕzh' ûr)	

LESSON CV. Some Household Duties.

frῦ' ĭng	fōld' ĭng	dŭst' ĭng	rōast' ĭng
băk' ĭng	cŭt' tĭng	pĭck' lĭng	knēad' ĭng
mĭn' çĭng	pēel' ĭng	elēan' ĭng	strāin' ĭng
boil' ĭng	rŭb' bĭng	knĭt' tĭng	sprĭn' klĭng
chŏp' pĭng	swēep' ĭng	tōast' ĭng	prĕ şẽrv' ĭng

LESSON CVI. A House and its Parts.

hạll	elŏş' ĕt	kĭtch' ĕn	vĕ răn' dȧ
house	păn' trῦ	eŏal' bĭn	stâir' eāse
stōop	bĕd' rōom	wạrd' rōbe	seŭl' lēr ў
pōrch	bȧth' rōom	lĭ' brȧ rῦ	stōre' rōom
ăt' tĭe	thrĕsh' ōld	eŭ' pȯ lȧ	pär' lor (-lēr)
găr' rĕt	pĭ ăz' zȧ	bāse' ment	dĭn' ĭng rōom
ĕn' trῦ	lăun' drῦ	băl' eȯ nῦ	elōtheş' prĕss

LESSON CVII. Kinds of Buildings.

ĭnn	tow' ēr (tou' ēr)	mēet' ĭng house
bärn	tăv' ẽrn	rĕs' tau (-tȯ) rànt
eŏurt	stȧ' ble	măn' or (-ēr) house
elŭb	mär' kĕt	pȧ vĭl' ion (pȧ vĭl' yŭn)
lŏdge	pŭb' lĭe house	măn' sion (măn' shŭn)

LESSON CVIII. Words relating to Sight.

sēe	pēep	dĕ serȳ'	view (vū)
spȳ	wạ*t*ch	rĕ gārd'	pĕr çĕive'
seăn	gāze	ĭn spĕet'	ĕ**x** ăm' ĭne
lŏŏk	glánçe	wĭt' nĕss	squint (skwĭnt)
wĭṉk	bĕ hōld'	ŏb ṣērve'	dĭṣ cērn' (-zērn)

LESSON CIX. Words relating to Eating and Drinking.

ĕat	fēast	tĭp' ple	gŏb' ble
sĭp	tāste	rĕ gāle'	ĭm bĭbe'
bīte	gôrġe	erä*u*nch	swạl' lŏ*w*
gŭlp	chōke	rĕl' ĭsh	chew (ch*ụ*)
gnạ*w*	drĭṉk	dĕ vour'	quaff (kwȧf';
dīne	mŭnch	nĭb' ble	măs' tĭ eāte

LESSON CX. On the Dinner table.

la' dle	dĕ eănt' ẽr	săl' *a*d bŏ*w*l'
năp' kĭn	wīne' gláss	tā' ble elŏth'
gŏb' lĕt	pīe' plate'	eärv' ĭng *k*nĭfe
eȧ rȧfe'	mēat' dĭsh	pīe' kle dĭsh'
*k*nĭfe' rĕst	grä'vȳ bōat	çĕl' ẽr ȳ gláss

LESSON CXI. Fruits.

fĭg	dăm' ṣon	strạ*w*' bĕr' rȳ
līme	mŭsk' mĕl' ȯn	gōōṣe' bĕr' rȳ
pru̱ne	răṣp' bĕr' rȳ	erăn' bĕr' rȳ
rā*i*' ṣĭn	blăck' bĕr' rȳ	hŭe' kle bĕr' rȳ

LESSON CXII. Nuts.

pĕ eăn'	ä*l*' mȯnd	hĭck' ȯ rȳ nŭt
a' eȯrn	bēech' nŭt	Mȧ dĕ*i*' rȧ nŭt
fĭl' bẽrt	chĕs*t*' nŭt	Brȧ zĭl' nŭt'
wạl' nŭt	hā' zel nŭt	eō' eȯ*a* nŭt'
pēa' nŭt	bŭt' tẽr nŭt'	shĕl*l*' bärk'

LESSON CXIII. Dictation.

Our mother sews, darns, knits, mends; she washes, irons, cleans, sweeps, and cooks; she watches, loves, and prays.

lóves	knĭts	eo͞oks	wạtch' ĕṣ
prȧys	mĕnds	swēeps	sews (sōṣ)
därns	elēans	wạsh' ĕṣ	ĭ' rons (ĭ' ŭrns)

LESSON CXIV. Water in Motion.

sûrf	tŏr' rent	eăt' á răet
wāve	răp' ĭds	break' ērṣ
bro͞ok	bĭl' lŏw	mĭll' rȧçé
flȯod	eăs eāde'	ŏ' cean (ŏ' shan)
rĭv' ēr	tĭde' wāve	show' ēr (shou'ēr)
frĕsh' ĕt	foun' taĭn	whirl' po͞ol' (hwĕrl'pool')

LESSON CXV. Air in Motion.

gŭst	çy͞' elōne	lê vănt' ēr
gāle	mŏn so͞on'	blĭz' zard (-zĕrd)
blȧst	tĕm' pĕst	squall (skwạl)
brēeze	tôr nä' dȯ	ty͞ pho͞on' (-fo͞on')
stôrm	sĭ rȯe' eȯ	zĕ' phyr (zĕf' ēr)
sĭ mo͞om'	hŭr' rĭ eāne	whirl' wĭnd' (hwĕrl' wĭnd')

LESSON CXVI. Vessels for holding Liquids.

jär	bŭtt	pĭp' kĭn	bŭck' ĕt
văt	flȧsk	skĭl' lĕt	pŭnch' eȯn
kĕg	erŏck	kĕt' tle	sạuçé' păn
tŭb	vĭ' al	pĭtch' ēr	dĕm' ĭ jŏhn
bōwl	bŏt' tle	çĭs' tĕrn	fir (-fĕr)' kĭn
eȧsk	bä' sĭn	eạl' drȯn	eär' boy (-boĭ)

LESSON CXVII. Dictation Exercise.

A cow moos, lows, bellows, and chews. A lamb bleats, baas, frisks, and gambols. A cat mews, purs, spits, and scratches. A chicken crows, clucks, lays, and cackles.

pûrş	mᴏᴏş	frĭsks	găm' bŏls
lāyş	bäaş	elŭcks	seră𝓁ch' ĕş
spĭts	blēats	eăe' kles	mews (mūz)
lᴏ𝑤ş	erᴏ𝑤ş	bĕl' lᴏ𝑤ş	chews (chụz)

LESSON CXVIII. Words meaning Occupation.

jŏb	pûr' sūĭt	vŏ eā' tion (-shŭn)
ärt	e𝑎𝓁𝓁 ĭng	sĭt ù ā' tion (-shŭn)
erăft	work (wûrk)	prŏ fĕs' sion (-fĕsh'ŭr)
trāde	busi' (bĭz-) nĕss	ĕm ploy' (-ploi') ment
bērth	ĕn gāge' ment	ŏe eū pā' tion (-shŭn)

LESSON CXIX.
Some words relating to Cleanliness and Dirt.

pūre	fĭl' thy̆	soiled	pŏl lūt' ĕd
foul	spŏt' lĕss	grĭm' y̆	ŏf fĕn' sĭve
grŏss	elĕan' ly̆	eōarse	dirt' y̆ (dēr' ty̆)
sprụçe	stain' lĕss	eŏr rŭpt'	ĭm măe' ū lāte
slĭm' y̆	ŭn sŭl' lĭed	smēared	tär' nĭshed (-nĭsht)

LESSON CXX. Occupations.

elĕrk	hŏs' 𝓁lēr	mēr' chant	tĕach' ēr
nûrse	eärv' ēr	plŭmb' ēr	wĕav' ēr
pŏr' tēr	mā' son	drŭg' gĭst	eā' tēr ēr
mĭn' ēr	bĭnd' ēr	sûr' ġeŏn	gär' den ēr
bär' bēr	färm' ēr	join' ēr	blăck' smĭth

LESSON CXXI. Boys and girls sometimes are

dŭl*l*	noiṣ' ў̆	băsh' fu̦l	pā' tient (pā' sh*e*nt)
-er*ŏ*s*s*	stū' pĭd	elŭm' ṣў̆	bois' tēr o*ŭ*s
ru̦d*e*	pla*y*' fu̦l	mĭrth' fu̦l ·	rê spēet' fu̦l
sĭn çēr*e*'	ŭn tĭ' dў̆	ŭn çĭv' ĭl	ĭm pēr' tĭ n*e*nt

LESSON CXXII. What a boy or girl should be.

kĭnd	*h*ŏn' ĕst	ô bē' dĭ *e*nt
gŏ͞od	joy' o*ŭ*s	stū' dĭ o*ŭ*s
frăn̤k	ēar' nĕst	ġĕn' ēr o*ŭ*s
brāv*e*	hōpe' fu̦l	ĕn ēr ġĕt' *le*
nō' ble	hĕlp' fu̦l	-eo*ŭ*r a' ġeo*ŭ*s
pô lĭt*e*'	tru̦th' fu̦l	ĭn dŭs' trĭ o*ŭ*s
hăp' pў̆	-eâr*e*' fu̦l	ăf fĕe' tion âte (-shŭn ăt)
lôv' ĭng	rĕv' ēr *e*nt	thought' fu̦l (th*a*t' fu̦l)

LESSON CXXIII. What a boy or girl should not be.

mēan	ärt' fu̦l	wĭ*c*k' ĕd
proud	stĭn' ġў̆	vĭ' cious (vĭsh' ŭs)
vā*i*n	sĕlf' ĭsh	spĭt*e*' fu̦l
la' zў̆	frĕt' fu̦l	dê çē*i*t' fu̦l
-eru̦' ĕl	prô fān*e*'	vŭl' gar (-gēr)
sŭlk' ў̆	ĭm pūr*e*'	-eow' ard lў̆ (-ērd lў̆)
sa̦*u*' çў̆	hēed' lĕs*s*	mȧ lĭ' cious (-lĭsh' ŭs)

LESSON CXXIV. Names of Boy*s*.

They should always begin with a capital letter.

Bēr' na̦rd	Fē' lĭx	Jô*h*n	Rĭch' a̦rd
Chärle̦ṣ	Frȧn' çĭs	Jō' sĕph	Rŏb' ērt
Dăn' ĭ ĕl	Ġeôrġe	La̦*w*' rĕnçe	Stē' ph*e*n (-v'n)
Ĕd' wa̦rd	Hĕn' rў̆	Lo̦*u*' ĭs	T*h*ŏm' a̦s
*E*ū' ġĕn*e*	Jāme̦ṣ	Nĭe*h*' ô la̦s	Wĭl' lia̦m (·ya̦m͗

LESSON CXXV. Dictation Exercise.

Our grocer sells bread, butter, tea, coffee, sugar, eggs, spices, crackers, ham, smoked beef, pickles, catchup, vinegar, molasses, sirup, apples, cider, potatoes, celery, prunes, canned goods, and other articles used on our tables.

tĕa	brĕad	eŏf′ fēe	är′ tĭ eles
hăm	spĭç′ĕş	ăp′ ples	pȯ tä′ tȯeş
ĕggş	bŭt′tĕr	erăck′ ērş	vĭn′ ê gar (-gēr)
çĭ′dēr	grō′çēr	pĭe′ kleş	sug′ ar (shŏŏg′ ēr)
sĭr′ŭp	prųnes	eăłch′ ŭp	smōked (smōkt) bēef
tä′ble	çĕl′ ēr ў	mȯ läs′ sĕş	eănned′ gŏŏdş

LESSON CXXVI. Nationalities.

Ĭ′ rĭsh	Chĭ′nĕşe′	En′ glĭsh (ĭn′ glĭsh)
Dŭłch	Jăp′ à nĕşe′	Ĭ tăl′ ĭan (-yan)
Swĭss	Aųs′ trĭ an	Prŭs′ sian (prŭsh′ an)
Frĕnch	Ȧ mĕr′ ĭ ean	Rŭs′ sian (rŭsh′ an)
Ġēr′ man	Ȧ rä′ bĭ an	Ā sĭ ăt′ ĭe (-shĭ ăt′ ĭe)
Spăn′ ĭsh	SĪ à mĕşe′	Ĭn′ dĭ an (-yan)
Hĭn′ dȯȯ	Ăf′ rĭ ean	Nŏr wē′ ġĭ an
Tûrk′ ĭsh	Ĕs′ kĭ mȯ	Eū rȯ pē′ an

LESSON CXXVII. Games.

pȯȯl	eûrl′ ĭng	tĕn′ pĭnş′	quoits (kwoits)
gŏlf	răck′ ĕts	fŏȯt′ ball′	lawn′ tĕn′ nĭs
chĕss	skĭt′ tleş	chĕck′ ērş	ġўm năs′ tĭes
pȯ′ lȯ	hȯck′ eў	sŏl′ ĭ tâire′	bĭl′ liardş(-yērdz)
ärch′ ēr ў	lĕap′ frȯg′	dŏm′ ĭ nȯeş	băck′ găm′ mȯn

LESSON CXXVIII   Words often Confounded.

lĕast, smallest.

lĕst, for fear that.

lĕeş, sediment; dregs.

lĕase, a letting of lands or buildings for a term of years.

mĭn' ute (mĭn' ĭt), sixty seconds.

mĭ nūte', very small.

Mōor, a native of northern Africa.

mōre, greater in any way.

pĭnt, half a quart.

point, the sharp end of a piercing instrument.

newş (nūz), a report of recent occurrences.

nōōşe, a running knot.

of (ŏv), from, out from.

ŏff, not on.

pō' ė sȳ, poetry.

pō' şȳ, a bouquet; a nosegay.

prŏf' ĭt, gain; benefit.

prŏph' ĕt, one who foretells events.

LESSON CXXIX.   Dictation Exercise.

Whatever you do for the least of men you do for God. Watch sharp lest the enemy find you sleeping. There is nothing left of the wine but the lees in the cask. We have taken a new lease of our house. The news of the accident contains even the most minute details. Wait for me; I shall not be more than a minute. The Moor, though quite dark, is not a negro. A quart will not go into a pint measure. I have broken the point of my pencil. The horse tried to throw off the noose, but it held him tight. Music and poesy go hand in hand. The girl gave a posy to her mother. No man is a prophet in his own country. The profit on some goods is large.

LESSON CXXX. Dictation Exercise.

A horse walks, runs, trots, paces, gallops, canters, races, kicks, neighs. A dog barks, growls, snarls, whines, snaps, bites, guards.

rŭns	bärks	rāç' ĕṣ	eăn' tērs
bītes	snärls	guärds	găl' lŏps
trŏts	kĭcks	nẹighs	growls (grouls)
snăps	wạlks	pāç' ĕṣ	whines (hwīnes)

LESSON CXXXI. On Colors.

Name the colors of the following:

skỹ	lĭ' ȯn	strạw	bŭt' tēr
rōṣe	blȯod	ŏl' īve	pīe' kles
gōld	pĕạṣ	lĕm' ȯn	pŭmp' kĭn
plŭm	spȯnġe	bụsh' ĕṣ	ĕm' ẽr ạld
brĭck	çŏ' dar (-dēr)	eȯp' pēr	gōōṣe' bĕr rỹ
grȧss	ĭn' dĭ gȯ	chĕr' rỹ	strạw' bĕr rỹ

LESSON CXXXII. Names of Boys.

Çē' çĭl	Ja' ẹọb	Ăm' brōṣe	Ạu gŭs' tŭs
Băṣ' ĭl	Ér' nĕst	Clĕm' ĕnt	Gŭs tā' vŭs
Çỹr' ĭl	Ĭ' ṣạae	Jĕr' ọme	Cŏr nē' lĭ ŭs
Ŏs' eạr	Hẽr' bẽrt	Păt' rĭck	Bĕn' ė dĭet
Är' thụr	Gĭl' bẽrt	Grĕg' ȯ rỹ	Fẽr' dĭ nănd

LESSON CXXXIII. Names of Girls.

Ē' dĭth	Ĭ rēne'	Ĕl' ė ȧ nȯr	Ăd' ė līne
Ĕm' mȧ	Ma' bĕl	Brĭdġ' ĕt	Cŏn' stạnçe
Lū' çỹ	Ė lĭ' zȧ	Ȧ mē' lĭ ȧ	Chär' lŏtte
Grāçe	Ăg' ȧ thȧ	Bė' ȧ trĭçe	Ġĕr' ạl dĭne
Mā' rỹ	Blȧnche	Bär' bȧ rȧ	Căth' ẽr ĭne

LESSON CXXXIV. Words having opposite meanings

vïçe	beaū' tў	dĕbt' or (-ēr)	ïn tŏl' ēr ant
fēar	eoŭr' âge	vīr' tûe	erĕd' ĭt or (-ēr)
grïĕf	lĭb' ēr al	hăp' pĭ nĕss	ạwk' ward (-wĕrd)
fïĕrçe	frēe' dòm	ŭg' lĭ nĕss	är' tĭ fĭ' cial(-fĭsh' al)
ġĕn' tle	slāv' ēr ў	grāçe' fụl	rė bĕl' lion (-yŭn)
mȧs' tēr	sĕrv' ạnt	năt' û ral	loy' (loi) ạl tў

LESSON CXXXV. The Cries of Animals.

Tell to which Animal each of the following cries belongs.

hĭss	rōar	blēat	elŭck
eạw	bärk	nẹigh	chăt' tēr
brāy	growl	quăck	gŏb' ble

LESSON CXXXVI. Words often mispronounced.

Pay particular attention to accented syllables.

a' eȯrn	eȯme' lў	rė çĕss'	sŏl' âçe
ȧ dŭlt'	erēa' tûre	dė' tail	ūṣ' âge
aġ' ĭle	dū' tў	seârçe	stăt' ûe
ăl lў'	gŏs' pĕl	ĭn quĭr' ў	heärth
çĭt' ĭ zen	grā' tĭs	mû ṣē' ŭm	fĭ nănçe'

LESSON CXXXVII. More words often mispronounced.

tăs' sel	eătch	prĕf' âçe	tĭ' nў
sạu' çў	bälm	sĭr' ŭp	rĭnse
yạcht	făç'ĕt	ĕn' gĭne	vĭe' ar (ēr)
dai' rў	äl' mȯnd	dĕaf	pĭ ä' nȯ

LESSON CXXXVIII.

Some words relating to heat and to cold

hŏt	blēak	äre' tĭe	flăm' ĭng
ĭ' çў	tĕp' ĭd	frĭg' ĭd	frēez' ĭng
eōld	kēen	frŏst' ў	glŏw' ĭng
wạrm	fĭ' ēr ў	blăz' ĭng	bûrn' ĭng

LESSON CXXXIX.

A Shoe is made of many parts, as follows:

sōle	tōe	thrĕad	ĭn′ stĕp
wĕlt	pĕgs	strĭngs	eoun′ tēr
hēel	tăgs	tòngue	bŭt′ tons
nāils	shăn̰k	eătch′ ĕş	eȳe′ lĕts
ŭp′ pēr	ĭn′ sōle	bĭnd′ ĭng	wăx′ ĕnd

LESSON CXL. Meats.

trĭpe	bā′ eon	brĭs′ kĕt	sĭr′ loin
joint	tòngue	shōul′ dēr	eôrned bēef′
round	ġĭb′ lĕts	knŭe′ kle	pōr′ tēr house
fĭl′ lĕt	kĭd′ neȳ	chŭck′ rĭb′	tĕn′ dēr loin′

LESSON CXLI. Parts of a Watch or Clock.

eŏg	hănd	sprĭng	wheel (hwĕl)
eāse	lē′ vēr	weight	jew′ ĕl (jū′ ĕl)
fāçe	rĭv′ ĕt	pĕn′ dù lŭm	rĕg′ ù lā′ tor (-tēr)
dĭ′al	pĭv′ ŏt	hâir′ sprĭng′	băl′ ançe wheel′ (-hwĕl)

LESSON CXLII. Words meaning to unite.

tĭe	stĭtch	bŭt′ ton	fàs′ ten
bĭnd	elĭnch	bŭe′ kle	här′ nĕss
bōlt	splĭçe	sê eūre′	ăt tăch′
tăck	rĭv′ ĕt	sew (sō)	gird (gērd)
brāid	elàsp	fix (fĭks)	sŏl′ dēr (sŏd′ēr)

LESSON CXLIII. Words meaning to separate.

teâr	sĕv′ ēr	shĭv′ ēr	rŭp′ tûre
rĕnd	sŭn′ dēr	dê tăch′	sĕp′ à rāte
breāk	bûrst	dĭ vĭde′	sĕg′ rê gāte
lōōse	dĭs sĕet′	dĭ v̆ôrçe′	dĭs′ eŏn nĕet′

LESSON CXLIV. Homonyms.

hĕar, to obtain knowl-
edge through the ear.

hĕre, in this place.

hĕrd, a drove.

hĕard, did hear.

hōle, a hollow place; a
pit.

whōle, all; complete.

ĭsle, an island.

aĭsle, a passage in a
church.

lĕss' en, to reduce; to
decrease.

lĕs' son, a task to be
learned or read.

quay (kē), a wharf; a
dock.

kēy, an instrument for
shutting and opening
a lock.

nō, a word of refusal.

knōw, to understand.

knew (nū), understood.

new (nū), lately done or
made.

gnū, a wild animal of
Africa.

măde, did make.

măid, an unmarried wo-
man.

LESSON CXLV. Dictation Exercise.

Let the pupils supply the missing words.

I want to hear the choir sing. The whole ——
of cattle ran away. The natives of the isle killed
the missionary. There is a crowd on the quay.
I was standing here when I heard a call, and
looking up saw the boy fall into the hole. Our
pew at church is in the middle ——. I know I
had a new —— made for the lock, but I cannot
find it. There are no titles in this country. The
little maid knew her lesson well. There is a gnu
in Central Park. Warm water will often lessen
the pain of a bruise.

LESSON CXLVI. Dictation Exercise.

A cabinet maker makes tables, chairs, bureaus, bedsteads, washstands, and bookcases.

A table has a frame, top, legs, and castors.

A chair has a seat, back, legs, rounds, and sometimes rockers. There are arm-chairs, rocking-chairs, camp-chairs, cane-chairs, and other kinds.

A bureau has a frame, drawers, and often a mirror.

A washstand has a drawer and a cup-board.

A bookcase has shelves and drawers.

LESSON CXLVII.

ärm	eămp	shĕlveş	wạsh' stănds
lĕgs	ŏf' ten	rŏck' ērş	mĭr' ror (-rēr)
eāne	dŏorş	drạw' ērş	eăb' ĭ nĕt măk' ēr
băck	frāme	sòme' tĭmeş	eŭp' board (kŭb' bērd)

LESSON CXLVIII.
Tell what article has the following parts.

dĭ' al	kēy	eāse	nŭm' bērş
hănds	fāçe	eŏgs	pĕn' dû lŭm
frāme	bĕll	sprĭngs	works (wûrks)
wẹights	chāin	hăm' mēr	wheels (hwēls)

LESSON CXLIX.
Articles of Personal Comfort or Convenience.

wạtch	nĭght' kēy	pär' â sŏl'	spĕe' tà eleş
pûrse	mătch' sāfe	ŭm brĕl' là	pŏck' ĕt bŏŏk
knĭfe	eȳe' glàss'	măck' ĭn tòsh	bŭt' ton hŏŏk'
pĕn' çĭl	slĭp' pērş	wạ' tēr prŏof	hănd' kēr chĭef
dĭ' â rў	eärd' ease	ŏ' vēr shọeş	mĕm ô răn' dŭm

LESSON CL. Common Contractions.

Supply the missing letters, and write in full the words from which the contractions are formed.

it's	you'll	isn't	'twas
he's	he'd	can't	'twasn't
let's	they'd	hasn't	didn't
I'll	we've	aren't	hadn't
he'll	you've	shan't	wouldn't
we'll	won't	you're	couldn't

LESSON CLI. Channels for Water.

pīpe	drāin	gŭl'lў	trough (trŏf)
dīke	spout	eŭl' vērt	sew' (sū'-) ēr
māin	slūiçe	fŭn' nĕl	sī' phon (-fŏn)
mōat	eà nȧl'	eŏn' duït	wāste' pīpe
dĭtch	gŭt' tēr	chăn' nĕl	aq' (ăk') ue (wê) dŭet

LESSON CLII. On Colors.

Name the colors of the following:

sŏŏt	shēet	snŭff	eŏf' fêe
līme	eŏal	cha̯lk	blăck' ĭng
erŏw	snŏw	sĭl' vēr	chŏe' ŏ lȧte

LESSON CLIII. Articles of Dress.

bĕlt	blouşe	măn' tle	ŏ' vēr eŏat
vĕst	frŏck	lĕg' gĭnş	mŏe' eà sĭns
eŏat	elŏak	mŭf' flēr	gäunt' lĕt
rŏbe	seärf	dŭst' ēr	wrĭst' band
săsh	tū' nĭe	pe lĭsse'	wāist' eŏat
eâpe	tĭp' pĕt	trou' şērş	pĕt' tĭ eŏat
vẹil	eŏr' sĕt	dra̯w' ērş	păn' tà lŏŏns
hŏŏd	bŏd' lçe	ŏ' vēr ạlⱡş	breech' êş (brĭch' ĕz)

LESSON CLIV. Things relating to a Book.

ĭṇk	prĭnt' ĭng	sĭdes	glūe
tȳpe	bĭnd' ĭng	eóv' ẽr	lĕath' ẽr
pā' pẽr	gĭld'ĭng	băck	lĭnes
păġ' ĕṣ	ĕdġ' ĕṣ	thrĕad	tī' tle
lĕaveṣ	lĭn' ĭng	păste	chăp' tẽr

LESSON CLV. Names of Boys.

Lūke	Dā' vĭd	Gā' brĭ ĕl	Mī' ehȧ ĕl
Nĕal	Phĭl' ĭp	Săm' ū ĕl	Măt' thew (măth' yu̜)
Pau̜l	Wa̱l' tẽr	Thē' ô dōre	Mau̜' rĭçe
Märk	Au̱s' tĭn	Tĭm' ô thў	Ăl' ĕx ăn' dẽr
Mĭleṣ	Ăl' frĕd	Ăn' thô nў	Bĕn' ja̱ mĭn
Dĕn' ĭs	Ăn' drew	Frĕd' ẽr ĭe	Chrĭs' tô phẽr (-fẽr)

LESSON CLVI.
The original States and their Abbreviations.

Vir (vẹr-) ġĭn' ĭ a̱,	Va.	Rhȯde Ĭs' la̱nd,	R. I.
New Yôrk',	N. Y.	Dĕl' a̱ wâre,	Del.
Măss a̱ chū' sĕtts,	Mass.	Nôrth Căr ô lĭ' na̱,	N. C.
New Hămp' shįre,	N. H.	New Jẽr' ṣeў,	N. J.
Cȯn nĕct' ĭ eŭt,	Conn.	South Căr ô lĭ' na̱,	S. C.
Mar' (mĕr-) ў la̱nd,	Md.	Pĕnn' sўl vā' nĭ a̱,	Pa.

Ġeôr' ġĭ a̱, Ga.

LESSON CLVII. Used in Letter-writing.

flў' lĕaf	pōst' serĭpt	ĕn' vĕl ōpe
è pĭs' tle	pōst' ôf' fĭçe	a̱u̱' tô gráph (-grȧf)
sûr' nāme	nōte' pā'pẽr	păr' ȧ grȧph (-grȧf)
ăd drĕss'	dè lĭv' ẽr ў	eôr rè spȯnd' ençe
hĕad' ĭng	sĭg' nȧ tûre	Chrĭs' tian (chan) nȧme

LESSON CLVIII. Names of God.

Dě' ı tỷ	Ạl mɪ*ght*' ў	Prŏv' ɪ dençe
Ĭn' fɪ nĭte	Rĕ dēem' ēr	Ŏm nĭp' ŏ tent
The Fä' thēr	The Mak' ēr	Ŏm' nɪ prĕş' ent
Ė tēr' nal	Sãv' ior (-yēr)	In' tēr çĕs' sor (-sēr)
Jĕ hŏ' vả*h*	Crĕ ả' tor (-tēr)	Sû prēme' Bĕ' ĭng
Á noint' ĕd	The Prĕ şērv' ēr	Mĕ' dĭ ả' tor (-tēr)

LESSON CLIX. Church Officers.

pŏpe	lĕg' åte	prɪ' måte	çĕl' ĕ brant
prɪēst	eṳ' råte	prĕl' åte	sŭb dēa' eon
dēan	bĭsh' ŏp	dēa' eon	ärch' bĭsh' ŏp
elĕr' ɪe	pŏn' tĭf*f*	ăe' ŏ lỷte	nŭn' cɪ ŏ (-shɪ ŏ)
lĕe' tŏr	elēr' ġỷ	eär' dɪ nal	vɪe' ar (-ēr) ġĕn' ēr al

LESSON CLX. Religious Offices and States.

nŭn	hēr' mɪt	g*u*ärd' ɪ an	ăl' mŏn ēr
mŏṇk	rĕ elûse'	frɪ' ar (-ēr)	ăṇ' e*h*ŏ rɪte
ăb' bŏt	pĕn' ɪ tent	prɪ' or (-ēr)	dɪ rĕet' or (-ēr)
ăb' bĕs*s*	pŏs' tû lant	rĕe'tor (-tēr)	sû pĕ' rɪ or (-ēr)
nŏv' ɪçe	sŏl' ɪ tå rỷ	lā*y*' brŏth' ēr	prŏ fĕs*s*ed' (-fĕst'*z*

LESSON CLXI. Words relating to Religion.

thrōn*e*s	chĕr' û bɪm	mär' tyrs (-tērs)
ăn' ġĕls	pã' trɪ äre*h*s	äre*h*' ăn' ġĕls
spɪr' ɪts	vɪr' tû*e*ş	sĕr' å phɪm (-fɪm)
å pŏs' *t*le*ş*	vɪr' ġɪns	eŏn fĕs*s*' ors (-ērs)
trɪn' ɪ tỷ	pow' (pou'-) ērş	dŏm ɪ nä' tions*
dɪ vɪn' ɪ tỷ	prŏph' (prŏf'-) ĕts	prɪn' çɪ păl' ɪ tɪe*ş*

---

* The pronunciation of the termination *tion* (shŭn) will be omitted from this out.

LESSON CLXII. Homonyms.

tŏe, part of the foot.

tŏw, coarse flax.

threw (thrụ), did throw.

thrọugh, from end to end or from one side to the other.

thêir, of them.

thêre, in that place.

vāne, a weather-cock.

vāin, fruitless; proud of little things.

vẹin, a blood-vessel.

tīde, stream; current.

tīed, made fast.

wāit, to stay for.

wẹight, a load; something heavy.

wāy, street; road.

wẹigh, to find the heaviness of.

wĕek, seven days.

wēak, not strong.

wŏod, the substance of a tree; a forest.

wọuld, the past tense of *will*.

yōke, that which connects or binds.

yŏlk, the yellow part of an egg.

LESSON CLXIII. Dictation Exercise.

Tow burns almost as quickly as gunpowder. If we should weigh the vane of the hall tower we would find its weight to be at least a hundred pounds. I cut a vein in my arm over a week ago, and still have to keep it tied up. It were vain for the slaves to rebel, as they are too weak to cast off their yoke. A wood fire looks cheerful. My brother's horse ran away, and threw him out of his carriage. The egg has a double yolk. Time and tide wait for no man. Where there is a will there is a way. I hurt my toe in walking through the dark room.

LESSON CLXIV. Words relating to Religion.

Bī' ble	serĭp' tûre	wòr' shĭp
gŏs' pĕl	pär' á ble	eòn' sê erāte
psäℓms	eän' tĭ ele	ŏb lä' tion
ăn' thĕm	mĭr' á ele	ăd' ô rā' tion
ê pĭs' ℓle	çĕl' ê brāte	săe' rĭ fĭce (fĭz)
fä' thêrş	çêr' ê mò nў	rê lĭ' ġiòn (-lĭj' ŭn)
trá dĭ' tion (-dĭsh' ŭn)		ŏf fĭ' cĭ āte (-fĭsh' I ät)

LESSON CLXV. Articles about the Altar.

pўx	çĕn' sēr	aℓ' tar (-tēr)	çĭ bō' rĭ ŭm
paℓℓ	erṳ' ĕts	erṳ' çĭ fĭx	tăb' ēr nà ele
bûrse	mĭs' sal	eôr' pò ral	ăn' tê pĕn' dĭ ŭm
păt' ĕn	chăl' ĭçe	mòn' strançe	pū' rĭ fĭ eâ' tor (-tēr)

LESSON CLXVI. Vestments.

ălb	mĭ' tēr	eăs' sòck	chăş' û ble
stōle	ăm' ĭçe	çĭne' tûre	dăl măt' ĭe
eōpe	păl' lĭ ŭm	sûr' plĭçe	gīr' dle
hăb' ĭt	măn' I ple	bĕr rĕt' tà	soṳ' táne'

LESSON CLXVII. More articles about the Altar.

stăt' ûe	aℓ' tar (-tēr) eärds	rĕl' ĭ quâ (-kwâ) rў
tä' pērş	ăb lū' tion eŭp	êx pô sĭ' tion (-zĭsh' ŭn)
erê' dençe	sĕp' ŭl eℏêr	păs' eℏal eän' dle
oil' stŏcks	eän dê lä' brà	săṇe' tû â rў lămp'

LESSON CLXVIII. Words relating to the Church.

dòg' mà	lĭt' ŭr ġў	ăp' ŏs tŏl' ĭe	aṳ thòr' ĭ tў
sўn' òd	hō' lĭ nĕss	prĭ' mà çў	ôe' û mòn' ĭe
û' nĭ tў	mĭl' ĭ tant	mўs' tĭe al	pēr' pĕt' û al
dŏe' trĭne	săṇe' tĭ tў	prĭm' ĭ tĭve	sû prêm' â çў
eoun'çĭl	sûf' fēr ĭng	ĭn fäl' lĭ ble	eăth' ô lĭç' ĭ tў

LESSON CLXIX.
More Trades, Occupations, and Professions.

sēam' strĕss   gōld' smĭth   jăn' ĭ tor (-tẽr)

ĕn' ġĭ nēer'   pẽr fûm' ẽr   seŭlp' tor (-tẽr)

mĭl' lĭ nẽr   ĕd' ĭ tor (-tẽr)   sûr vęy'or (-ẽr)

eär' pĕn tẽr   ạu' thor (-thẽr)   hĭs tō' rĭ ạn

drĕss' māk' ẽr   mû si'cian (-zĭsh' ạn)

stä' tion ẽr   phy sĭ'cian (fĭ zĭsh' ạn)

LESSON CLXX. Public Officers.

shĕr' ĭf   pô lïçe' man   gòv' ẽrn or (-ẽr)

tûrn' kēy   eòn' stȧ ble   eŏl lĕet' or (-tẽr)

wạrd' ẹn   māy' or (ẽr)   ĭn spēet'or (-tẽr)

prĕṣ'ĭ dẹnt   măġ' ĭs trȧte   ăs sĕss' or (-sẽr)

ạl' dẽr mạn   sĕn' ȧ tor (-tẽr)   ăs sĕm' blў mạn

trĕaṣ' (trĕzh'-) ûr ẽr   eŏm mĭs' sion (-mĭsh ŭn-) ẽr

LESSON CLXXI. Parts of the Body.

skĭn   heärt   fĭ' bẽr   măr' rōw

bōne   brăin   lĭv' ẽr   är' tẽr ў

vęin   joint   tŏn' sĭl   knŭe' kle

rĭbs   blòod   gŭl' lĕt   wĭnd' pĭpe'

flĕsh   nẽrve   mŭs' cle   sĭn' ew (-û)

skŭll   lŭngs   păl' ȧte   stòm' ạeh

seălp   glănd   nŏs' trĭl   lăr' ўnx

LESSON CLXXII. Relating to Painting.

brŭsh   ēa' ṣel   eăn' vas   chär' eŏal

păint   păl' lĕt   vär' nĭsh   tăp' ĕs trў

skĕtch   stŭd' ў   out' lïne   dĭs tĕm' pẽr

pĕn' çĭl   frĕs' eô   eär tōon'   lănd' seạpe

păs' tĕl   erāy' ȯn   pŏr' trȧit   mĭn' ĭ ȧ tûre

LESSON CLXXIII. Words relating to History.

ăg̍' ĕş	stătes	pró fāne'	nā' tions (-shŭns)
ĕp' ŏeʜs	ryl' ērş	lĕad' ērş	çĕn' tû rĭeş
mŏd' ērn	eŭs' tòms	ġĕn' ēr al	gòv' ērn ments
sā' erĕd	dĕe' ȧdes	măn' nērş	ăn' cient (-shent)

LESSON CLXXIV.
Words frequently mispronounced or improperly accented.

dĕaf	dŭ' tў	răp' ĭne	prĕf' ȧçe
ĕ' vɩl	ɩ dĕ' ȧ	frăġ' ĭle	ôr' dê al
ŏf' ten	dŏç' ĭle	rĕs' pĭte	fī nănçe'
făç' ĕt	lĕġ' ĕnd	jŏe' ŭnd	hò rī' zȯn
ā mĕn'	prŏ' fīle	prŏç' ĕss	mû şĕ' ŭm
heärth	eou' pȯn	eŏl' ŭmn	ŏp pŏ' nent

LESSON CLXXV. Words used in Arithmetic.

plŭs	ĭn' tê ġēr	ăn' swēr	fīg' ûres
eūbe	Ār' ȧ bɩe	eŏm pūte'	prŏd' ŭet
ʒhōle	eăn' çĕl	nŭm' bērş	făe' tor (-tēr)
mĭ'nŭs	prŏb' lĕm	ĭn erŏase'	mĭxed (mĭkst)
Rŏ' man	ȧ mount'	dê erŏase'	squâre (skwâr)

LESSON CLXXVI. More words used in Arithmetic.

mŭl' tɩ ple	frăe' tion	sŭb' trȧ hĕnd
dĕç' ɩ mal	nó tȧ' tion	mŭl' tɩ plɩ eănd'
dĭv' ɩ dĕnd	prŏ pŏr' tion	ăl' ɩ quot (-kwŏt)
eŏm' pound	sŭb trăe' tion	dɩ vi' sion (-vĭzh' ŭn)
mĭn' û ĕnd	nŭ mēr ā' tion	nŭ' mēr ā tor (-tēr)
rê maɩn' dēr	dɩ vɩ' şor (-zēr)	dê nŏm' ɩ nā tor (tēr)
quŏ' tient (kwŏ' shĕnt)		ăd dɩ' tion (-dĭsh' ŭn)

LESSON CLXXVII. Words often Confounded.

ăe çĕss', admission; entrance.

ĕx' çĕss', more than enough.

ĕx' ĕr çĭşe, exertion; employment.

ĕx' ŏr çĭşe, to drive away an evil spirit.

ĕast, the point where the sun rises.

yĕast, a preparation used for raising dough.

ê lĭç' ĭt, to draw out; to bring to light.

ĭl lĭç' ĭt, unlawful.

ĕm' ĭ nençe, high rank; exalted.

ĭm' mĭ nençe, a threatening; a something near at hand.

ê rŭp' tion; a violent throwing out of flames.

ĭr rŭp' tion; violent entrance of invaders.

LESSON CLXXVIII. Dictation Exercise.

The soldier attempted to gain access to the barracks. Avoid excess of any kind. Moderate exercise contributes to health. The bishop at once proceeded to exorcise the evil spirit. The east is in a blaze of light this morning. The baker did not use enough yeast in the bread. The judge could elicit no information from the prisoner. The police found an illicit distillery in an old barn with a number of men at work. Cardinal Newman reached a great eminence as a writer of pure English. There is imminence of great danger in the careless handling of powder. In the year 79 there was an eruption of Mt. Vesuvius. About the year 420 the Franks made an irruption into Gaul.

LESSON CLXXIX. Words relating to Holiness.

hŏ′ lў	gŏd′ lў	dê vŏt′ ĕd	sȧint′ lў
pī′ oŭs	hŭm′ ble	spĭr′ ĭt ŭ ạl	ĕd′ ĭ fў′ ĭng
dê vout′	rĕv′ ēr ent	rê lĭ′ ġioŭs	rĭght′ eous (-chŭs)

LESSON CLXXX.
Some words relating to Health and to Sickness.

wĕll	hĕalth	ĭll′ nĕss	dê erĕp′ ĭt
hāle	sound	wĕak′ lў	măl′ ȧ dў
här′ dў	rŏ bŭst′	sĭck′ nĕss	dĕl′ ĭ eȧte
heärt′ ў	vĭg′ or (-ēr)	ȧil′ ment	ĭn fĭrm′ ĭ tў

LESSON CLXXXI.
Some words relating to Danger and to Safety.

rĭsk	shĭĕld	sȧfe′ tў	sê eūr′ ĭ tў
pĕr′ ĭl	dăn′ ġēr	vĕn′ tŭre	hăz′ ard (-ērd)
	prŏ tĕe′ tion		prĕş ēr vȧ′ tion

LESSON CLXXXII. Titles applied to Books.

tāle	lĕg′ ĕnd	trēat′ ĭse	năr′ rȧ tĭve
stŏ′ rў	joûr′ nạl	ăn′ ĕe dōte	mĕm′ oir (-wŏr)
ĕs′ sȧy	hĭs′ tŏ rў	ăd vĕn′ tŭre	bĭ ŏg′ rȧ phy (-fў)

LESSON CLXXXIII. Words used in Grammar.

vêrb	nŭm′ bēr	prĕd′ ĭ eȧte
eāse	ăd′ vêrb	phrȧşe (frās)
noun	sŭb′ jĕet	ȧ năl′ ў sĭs
tĕnse	sĕn′ tençe	eŏn jŭṇe′ tion
mood	pärs′ ĭng	ĭn flĕe′ tion
voiçe	är′ tĭ ele	ĭn′ tēr jĕe′ tion
elause	ăd′ jŭṇet	pŭṇe′ tŭ ā′ tion
ġĕn′ dēr	prŏ′ noun	eŏn′ jû gā′ tion
pĕr′ son	ăd′ jĕe tĭve	prĕp′ ŏ sĭ′ tion (-zĭsh′ ŭn)

LESSON CLXXXIV. Synonyms.

These words are to be distinguished carefully from one another.

glory
honor

Glory urges to extraordinary efforts and great undertakings; *honor* leads to a discharge of one's duty. *Glory* is for the few only; *honor* is more or less within the reach of all. A nation gains *glory* by the splendor of its victories; *honor*, by the justice and generosity of its government.

great
large
big

Great is applied to all kinds of dimensions in which things can grow or increase; *large* is properly applied to space, extent, and quantity; *big* denotes great as to expansion or capacity. A house, a room, an army may be called *great* or *large;* an animal or a mountain is *large* or *big.* For example, a *great* farm, a *large* lake, a *big* dog.

genius
talent

Genius is born with a man, a gift of nature; *talent* supposes a peculiar aptitude for certain employments and ends and purposes. It requires a *genius* for poetry, for a man to be a poet; it requires a *talent* to learn languages.

generous
liberal

Generous signifies high-born, and expresses that nobleness of soul which consults the feelings and happiness of others. *Liberal* means free-born, and implies largeness of spirit in giving, judging, acting, etc. A *generous* man will yield his claims when the relief of another is in question. A *liberal* spirit does not ask the reason for giving, but gives when the occasion offers.

gather
collect

Gather means merely to bring to one spot; *collect,* while it means to gather, also gives the idea of forming into a whole, as, we *gather* that which is scattered ; we *collect* rare books.

LESSON CLXXXV. Words used in Geography.

zōne	nôrth	stĕppe	tŏr' rĭd
ĕarth	south	plä' nèt	frĭg' ĭd
ĕast	glōbe	ĭs' land	trŏp' ĭe
wĕst	world (wûrld)	ĭs*th*' mŭs	ăre' tĭe

LESSON CLXXXVI.

Names of the States and Territories and their Abbreviations.

Begin each with a capital letter.

Vẹr mŏnt',	Vt.	Wĭs eŏn' sĭn,	Wis.
Kĕn tŭck' ў,	Ky.	Căl ĭ fôr' nĭ ạ,	Cal.
Tĕn' nẹs sē*e*',	Tenn.	Mĭnn e sŏ' tạ,	Minn.
Ō hī' ŏ,	Ohio.	Ŏr' ẹ gŏn,	Oreg.
Ĭn dĭ ăn' ạ,	Ind.	Kăn' sạs,	Kans.
Mĭss' ĭss ĭp' pĭ,	Miss.	Wĕst Vir gĭn'ĭ ạ,	W. Va.
Ĭl lĭ nois',	Ill.	Nẹ vä' dạ,	Nev.
Ăl' ạ bä' mạ,	Ala.	Nẹ brᴬs' kạ,	Nebr.
Maíne,	Me.	€ŏl ọ rä' dŏ,	Colo.
Mĭss ọu' rĭ,	Mo.	Nôrth Dạ kō' tạ,	N. Dak.
Ăr' kăn sạs,	Ark.	South Dạ kō' tạ,	S. Dak.
Mĭch' ĭ gạn,	Mich.	Mŏn tä' nạ,	Mont.
Flŏr' ĭ dạ,	Fla.	Wạsh' ĭng tọn,	Wash.
Tĕx' ạs,	Tex.	Ĭ' dạ hŏ,	Idaho.
Ĭ ó' wạ,	Iowa.	Wȳ ŏ' mĭng,	Wyo.

Lọu' i si (-è zè) ä' nạ,   La.

Ū' tä*h*,	Utah.	Ăr ĭ zō' nạ,	Ariz.
Ȧ läs' kạ,	Alaska.	Ŏk lä hō' mạ,	

Ĭn' dĭ ăn Tĕr' rĭ tò rȳ, '   Ind. T.

New Mĕx' i (-sĭ) €ŏ,   N. Mex.

Dĭs' trĭet òf €ò lŭm' bĭ ạ,   D. C.

LESSON CLXXXVII. Divisions of Land.

eäpe	hĭll	plà teau' (tò')	ĭsth' mŭs
plaın	văl' leў	moun' taĭn	är ehĭ pĕl' à gỏ
eðast	Ăf' rĭ eạ	Ä' si ạ (-shĭ ạ)	Nôrth Á mĕr' ĭ eạ
ĭs' land	Eu' ròpe	pĕn ĭn' sù là	South Á mĕr' ĭ eạ
Ĕast' ẽrn Cŏn' tĭ nent		Wĕst' ẽrn Cŏn' tĭ nent	

LESSON CLXXXVIII. A few words hard to spell.

rhĕt' ô rĭe	lăb' ŏ rà tô rў	plă' ġià rĭze
rà păç' ĭ tў	mĭs' dê mẽan' or (-ẽr)	seŭr' rĭl oŭs

LESSON CLXXXIX. Some words used in Geography.

elĭ'màte	rê pŭb' lĭe	trĭb' û tà rў
ĕm' pĭre	tĕm' pẽr åte	lŏn' ġĭ tūde
hô rĭ' zòn	păr' al lĕl	prŏm' òn tô rў
kĭng' dòm	lăt' ĭ tūde	ê qua' tor (-kwä' tẽr)
ĕs' tù å rў	mê rĭd' ĭ an	hĕm' ĭ sphere (-sfẽr)

LESSON CXC. Names of Cities.
Begin each with a capital letter.

Păr' ĭs	Lòn' dòn	St. Lọu' ĭs	Bạl' tĭ mọre
Bẽr' lĭn	New Yôrk'	Brŏŏk' lўn	Çĭn' çĭn nä' tĭ
Bôs' tòn	Çhĭ eạ' gŏ	Lў' ọnş	Phĭl' ạ dĕl' phĭ ạ
Caır' ô	Vĭ ĕn' nạ	Lĭv' ẹr pŏŏl	St. Pẽ' tẹrş bûrg
Cän' tọn	Brŭs' sẹlş	Mĕl' boûrne	Săn Frăn çĭs' eŏ

LESSON CXCI. Names of Rivers.
Begin each with a capital letter.

Hŭd' sọn	Mĭss ọu' rĭ	Dĕl' à wâre	Yĕl' lŏw stŏne
Ō hĭ' ŏ	Ŏt' tạ wạ	Cô lŭm' bĭ ạ	Cŭm' bẹr land
Plătte	Pŏ tŏ' mạe	Är' kạn sạs	St. Lạw' rẹnçe
St. Jŏhn	Rŏ' ạ nŏke	Rĭ ô Grän' de	Mĭss' ĭss ĭp' pĭ
Wạ' bạsh	Nĭ ăg' ạ rạ	Ăl le ghä' nў	Sŭs' que hăn nạ)

LESSON CXCII. Common Abbreviations—Titles.

To be written from dictation.

Abp. is used for Archbishop		Ed. is used for Editor	
Bp. " " Bishop		Esq. " " Esquire	
Bro. " " Brother		Gen. " " General	
Capt. " " Captain		Gov. " " Governor	
Col. " " Colonel		H.H. " " His Holiness	
Dr. " " Doctor		Hon. " " Honorable	

D.D. is used for Doctor of Divinity

LESSON CXCIII. Common Abbreviations.

Ans., answer.

A. B., bachelor of arts.

Acct., account.

A. D., in the year of our Lord.

A. M., before noon.

Amt., amount.

Bbl., barrel.

B. V. M., Blessed Virgin Mary.

Cent. (*Centum*), a hundred.

Co., county.

Cor. Sec., corresponding secretary.

Cts., cents.

Cwt., a hundredweight.

Dept., department; deputy.

Disct., discount.

Do. (*Ditto*), the same.

Doz., dozen.

Ea., each.

LESSON CXCIV. Derivations.
Verbs formed from Nouns.

thrĭft	thrīve	clŏth	clōthe
brĕath	brēathe	ăc′ çĕnt	ăc çĕnt′
blŏod	blēed	eŏn′ flĭet	eŏn flĭet′
wrēath	wrēathe	eŏn′ tràst	eŏn tràst′
hälf	hälve	ĭn′ çĕnse	ĭn çĕnse′
gōld	gĭld	ĭn′ crēase	ĭn crēase′
bàth	bàthe	prĕs′ ent	prē sĕnt′

LESSON CXCV. Capital Letters.

1. The names of the Deity must begin with a capital letter ; as,

Our Savior, The Redeemer, The Almighty, etc.

2. The first word of every sentence must begin with a capital letter ; as,

I am learning to spell. Be kind to the poor.

3. The first word of every line in poetry must begin with a capital letter; as,

Great love through smallest channels will find its surest way;
It comforts and it blesses, hour by hour and day by day.

4. All proper names and nouns or adjectives formed from proper names, must begin with a capital ; as,

America, Christian, Mary, Sunday, July.

5. Titles of honor, office, and respect begin with a capital letter ; as,

His Holiness, Pope Leo XIII.

6. The first word of every direct quotation, example, precept, or question must begin with a capital letter ; as,

Remember the old proverb, "Well begun is half done."

7. The important words in the title of a book or essay, and also the heads of chapters and articles should begin with a capital ; as,

The New Second Reader. A Mexican Legend.

8. The words *I* and *O* must be written or printed in capitals; as,

Stopping, he cried, "O, Luke, I have lost the money!"

9. Names of things personified must begin with a capital letter ; as,

Grim Winter, in his snowy cloak, is here.

LESSON CXCVI. Synonyms.

These words are to be distinguished carefully from one another.

hinderance
impediment
obstacle

A *hinderance* is something that holds us back, but we break away from it; an *impediment* really entangles our feet, and we remove it; an *obstacle* rises before us in our way, and we surmount it.

grave
serious

Grave does not merely mean an absence of mirth, but a heaviness of mind which is shown in a man's walk, in his voice, in his gestures, and in his looks. *Serious* expresses the quality of slowness and indicates simply steadiness of action and a suppression of anything like jesting. Misfortune or age will produce *gravity; seriousness* is the result of reflection. Thus, we say, a *grave* assembly of old men; a *serious* discourse.

haste
hurry

Haste and *hurry* both imply quickness in movement and action, but while *haste* may be made with some design, *hurry* always supposes disorder, confusion, and irregularity. Men may make *haste*, children *hurry*.

ignorant
illiterate

Ignorant signifies want of information in general, or of knowledge of some particular subject; *illiterate* refers to want of knowledge acquired by reading and study. For example, many of the Crusaders were *illiterate*, but most of them were far from *ignorant* of the art of war.

industrious
diligent

We are *industrious* when steadily employed in laboring for some valuable end; we are *diligent* when we apply ourselves earnestly for some purpose which strongly interests us. The *diligent* man is contented with the employment he has; the *industrious* man goes from one employment to another.

LESSON CXCVII. Plants.

bŭd	bŭlb	vīne	blŏs' sŏm
bush	wēed	sprĭg	săp' lĭng
trēe	brȧnch	shrŭb	flow' er (flou' ẽr)

LESSON CXCVIII. Land.

mōōr	knōll	eȯast	ĭs' land
eȧpe	blŭff	mound	mĕad' ȯw
glĕn	eȯpse	fŏr' ĕst	pȧs' tūre
grŏve	swạmp	rȧ vīne'	moun' taĭn
mȧrsh	thĭck' ĕt	gär' den	eȧñ' ȯn (yŭn)

LESSON CXCIX. Harness.

gĭrth	eȯl' lar (-lẽr)	săd' dle	mär' tĭn gȧle
hȧme	blĭnd' ẽr	trȧç' ĕ§	rẹin' snăp'
hạl' tẽr	eûrb' bĭt'	stĭr' rŭp	chŏck' rẹin'

LESSON CC. Kinds of Conveyance.

gĭg	stȧġe	bŭg' gў	ŏm' nĭ bŭs
eăb	eȯach	sŭlk' ў	rŏck' ȧ wȧy
slĕd	slẹigh	eŭt' tẽr	vė lŏç' ĭ pĕde
drȧy	slĕdġe	eȧr' rў ạll'	bĭ' çў ele
eȧrt	çhāiṣe	eȧr' rĭaġe	eọu' pé (-pȧ')
trŭck	wăg' ȯn	bȧ rọụçhé'	phȧ' ė tŏn (fā'ė tŏn)

LESSON CCI. Highways and Byways.

lȧne	brĭdġe	ăv' ė nŭe	rȧĭl' rȯad'
strēet	cȧ năl'	tûrn' pĭke	vī' ȧ dŭet
eȯurt	fĕr' rў	pȧs' sȧġe	bọụ' lė vȧrd

LESSON CCII. Kinds of Vessels.

shĭp	jŭnk	eŭt' tẽr	shȧrp' ĭe
brĭg	yạwl	găl' leў	sehōōn' ẽr
bȧrk	yạcht	lŭg' gẽr	eȧt' ȧ mȧ răn'
slōōp	eȧ nọe'	pĭn' nȧçe	mŏn' ĭ tor (-tẽr)

LESSON CCIII. Singulars and Plurals.

The plurals of nouns regularly end in *s*, or, in certain classes of words in *es*.

A noun which ends in the singular with such a sound that the sound of *s* can unite with it and be pronounced without forming a separate syllable, forms its plural by adding *s* only.

trēe	trēeş	dwạrf	dwạrfs
bĕll	bĕlls	mȯn' eў	mȯn' eўş
ĕar	ĕarş	tûr' keў	tûr' keўş
prōof	prōofs	bär' gain (gĕn)	bär' gains (gĕns)

LESSON CCIV. Plurals.

Some nouns ending in *o* preceded by a consonant form their plurals by adding *es*.

ĕeh'ȯ	ĕeh'ȯeş	mŏt' tȯ	mŏt' tȯeş
eär' gȯ	eär' gȯeş	pȯ tä' tȯ	pȯ tä' tȯeş

LESSON CCV. Plurals.

Nouns ending in *y* preceded by a consonant form their plurals by adding *es* and changing *y* into *i*.

skȳ	skīeş	bā' bў	bā' bīeş
flȳ	flīeş	lā' dў	lā' dīeş
pō' nў	pō' nīeş	stō' rў	stō' rīeş
bŏd' ў	bŏd' īeş	är' mў	är' mīeş
pär' tў	pär' tīeş	eăn' dў	eăn' dīeş

LESSON CCVI. Plurals.

A few nouns ending in *f* or *fe* form their plurals by changing *f* or *fe* into *ves*.

lēaf	lēaveş	wīfe	wīveş
eälf	eälveş	knīfe	knīveş
wǫlf	wǫlveş	hälf	hälveş

LESSON CCVII. Synonyms.

These words are to be distinguished carefully from one another.

continuous
continual
constant
Continuous is used when the action is not interrupted; *continual* is that which is con-stantly renewed, with perhaps frequent inter-ruptions; *constant* means fixed, unchangeable; as, a *constant* mind; a *continuous* train of thought, a *continuous* flow of water; it rained *continually* during the day.

crime
sin
vice
Crime is a violation of human law; *sin* is an offense against God; *vice* is an offense against morality. For example, murder is a *crime* that is punished by death; it is also a *sin* which God will punish; idleness, if long continued, becomes a *vice*.

conduct
behavior
Conduct is the manner in which we act in the concerns of life; *behavior* refers to the mode in which we bear ourselves in the presence of others; as, the girl's *behavior* at school is all that can be desired; the man's *conduct* will be his ruin.

cheerful
gay
Cheerful marks an unruffled flow of spirits; *gay* is connected with joy. *Cheerfulness* is an habitual state of the mind; *gayety* depends on external circumstances. Thus, a *cheerful* countenance remains *cheerful; gayety* passes away as quickly as the pleasure which occasions it.

compulsion
constraint
Compulsion is the force applied by another to make us act against our will; *constraint* prevents us from acting according to our wishes. *Compulsion* is always produced by some active agent; *constraint* may be laid upon us by the forms of society or by other circumstances.

LESSON CCVIII. Words relating to small size.

wēe	tī' nў	pўg' mў	shrŭnk' en
shôrt	lĭt' tle	mĭ nūte'	ŭn' dĕr sīzed'
squạt	pĕt' tў	à tŏm' ĭe	dĭ mĭn' ŭ tīve
smạll	pū' nў	dwạrfed	mĭ erò seŏp' ĭe
mīte	dăp' pēr	frăg' ment	lĭl' lĭ pū' tian (-shạn)

LESSON CCIX. Titles.

jŭdġe	Hŏn'. or (ēr)	Rĕv' ēr end	€ăr' dĭ nạl
Grāçe	Māу' or (ēr)	Hō' lĭ nĕss	Ĕm' ĭ nençe
Pōpe	Măd' am	Gòv' ērn or (-ēr)	Ärch' bĭsh' òp
Mĭs' tēr	Mĭs' trĕss	Prĕṣ' ĭ dĕnt	Ĕx' çĕl lẹn çў

LESSON CCX. Titles of Respect.
(The abbreviations are in parenthesis.)

In addressing any one we ought to be particular to give him his proper title.

When we speak to the Pope we must say, *Your Holiness* cr *Holy Father;* to a Cardinal, *Your Eminence;* to an Archbishop, *Your Grace;* to a Bishop, *Right* (Rt.) *Reverend* (Rev.) Bishop; to a Priest, *Reverend Father* or *Reverend Sir.* In speaking to a Brother or a Sister of a religious Order we should say *Reverend Brother* or *Reverend Sister.*

When we address the head of our government we should say *Mister* (Mr.) *President;* the Governor of a State or Territory, *Your Excellency;* the Mayor of a city, *Your Honor* or *Mister Mayor;* a judge, *Your Honor.*

In addressing a gentleman we say *Mister;* to a married lady we say *Madam* or *Mistress* (pronounced *Missis* and abbreviated Mrs.); to an un-married lady, *Miss.*

LESSON CCXI. Words often Confounded.

ĕm' ĭ grāte, to remove from one country to another.

ĭm' mĭ grātc, to remove into a country.

fôr' mēr lў, in time past.

fôrm' ȧl lў, regularly; precisely.

grĭ$'lў, horrible; terrible.

grĭs' flў, like gristle.

hŭ$ $är', a horse-soldier.

hŭz zä', a shout of joy; hurrah.

hā' lŏ, a circle of light; a glory.

hăl' lŏw, to make holy.

ĭn ġĕn' ioŭs (-yŭs), skillful to invent.

ĭn ġĕn' ů oŭs, artless.

lĭn' ĭ ment, a kind of soft ointment.

lĭn' ė ȧ ment, form; feature.

lōose, free; not close.

lọ$e, to part with unintentionally.

LESSON CCXII. Dictation Exercise.

The poor family prepared to emigrate from Ireland, intending to immigrate to America. The meeting was formally opened by the chairman. The word grisly was formerly more in common use than it now is. The meat is gristly, and it is almost impossible to chew it. The hussar galloped to the front, and at sight of the enemy gave a loud huzza. In a picture a saint is generally represented with a halo around his head. Let us hallow the name of God. The time lock used in many banks is an ingenious contrivance. The lad has an ingenuous countenance; honesty is marked on every lineament of his face. Liniment is used to relieve wounds and bruises. My new coat is too loose. Be careful or you may lose your purse.

LESSON CCXIII. Synonyms.

These words are to be distinguished carefully from one another.

impracticable That is *impracticable* which cannot be done
impossible   by human skill ; that is *impossible* which is
                contrary to the laws of nature. For
                example, the navigation of a river may be
                impracticable in its present state, but it is
                not *impossible* that the obstructions may be
                removed, so as to make it navigable.

indigence   *Indigence* implies extreme distress, and almost
poverty   absolute destitution ; *poverty* denotes that
                state in which we are unable to provide
                ourselves with the conveniences of life.
                What would be *poverty* to some would be
                a sufficiency to others.

instant   *Instant* expresses a much shorter space of
moment   time than *moment; instant* is always taken
                for the present time ; *moment* for past,
                present, or future time. A dutiful child
                comes the *instant* he is called ; a prudent
                man embraces the favorable *moment.* One
                may say, a few *moments*, but not a few
                instants.

join   *Join* signifies to bring into close contact :
unite   *unite* implies to make into one. We *join*
                two houses together : people are *united* who
                are one in opinion, sentiment, condition,
                or circumstances.

indignation *Indignation* denotes the strong feeling which
resentment   unworthy conduct on the part of others
                excites in our hearts. *Resentment* is the feel-
                ing awakened by a deep sense of injury; it
                leads us to dislike the offenders as much as
                the offense, and to seek for a means of in-
                flicting pain in return.

LESSON CCXIV. Some Anglo-Saxon Verbs

sẽe	hōld	tĕll	thrōw
buȳ	gĭve	bĕat	mōurn
àsk	eòme	stănd	breăk
rŭn	dâre	knōw	chōoşe
rōw	sĭng	slēep	bê gĭn′
plăy	fĭnd	shīne	hew (hū)
hĕlp	eạll	knĕad	work (wûrk)
lĭve	bôrn	strīke	brew (brų)
tăke	wēep	strĕtch	plow (plou)

LESSON CCXV. Words spelled in two ways.

ax	axe	defense	defence
adz	adze	burden	burthen
clew	clue	mamma	mama
jail	gaol	inquire	enquire
vial	phial	wagon	waggon
plow	plough	peddler	pedlar
draft	draught	license	licence
bark	barque	whisky	whiskey

LESSON CCXVI. More words spelled in two ways.

burned	burnt	libeled	libelled
resin	rosin	gayety	gaiety
meter	metre	fullness	fulness
until	untill	entreaty	intreaty
theater	theatre	mustache	moustache
intrust	entrust	skillful	skilful
gray	grey	licorice	liquorice
cigar	segar	envelope	envelop

LESSON CCXVII. Words relating to Large Size.

bĭg	stout	màss′ ў	ĭm mĕnse′
tặll	plŭmp ·	màss′ ĭve	stạl′ wart (-wẽrt)
greāt	bûr′ lў	ăm′ ple	eȧ pä′ cious (-shŭs)
hūġe	pŏrt′ lў	mĭgħt′ ў	ġĭ găn′ tĭe
lärġe	bŭlk′ ў	cȯ lŏs′ sal	ė nȯr′ moŭs

LESSON CCXVIII. Words relating to Time.

ăġe	mȯnth	pŏ′ rĭ ȯd	ė tẽr′ nĭ tў
daу	ĕ′ rȧ	ĭn′ tẽr ĭm	fû tū′ rĭ tў
yĕar	ĕp′ ȯeħ	çĕn′ tû rў	tĕm′ pȯ rȧ rў
wĕek	dĕe′ ȧde	prĭm′ ĭ tĭve	eȯn tĕm′ pȯ rȧ rў

LESSON CCXIX. Used on a Farm.

räke	scȳthe	sĭe′ kle	pĭtch′ fȯrk
plow	eōlt′ ẽr	rēap′ ẽr	häу′ rĭck
flaĭl	mōw′ ẽr	prụn′ ẽr	häу′ eŭt′ tẽr
spāde	hăr′ rȯw	thrăsh′ ẽr	eŭl′ tĭ vä′ tor

LESSON CCXX. Farm-work.

häу′ ĭng	wēed′ ĭng	rēap′ ĭng	shŏck′ ĭng
sōw′ ĭng	tĭll′ ĭng	mōw′ ĭng	thrăsh′ ĭng
plănt′ ĭng	dĭtch′ ĭng	erä′ dlĭng	wĭn′ nȯw ĭng
hȯe′ ĭng	draĭn′ ĭng	bĭnd′ ĭng	här′ vĕsṭ ĭng

LESSON CCXXI. Some Anglo-Saxon Nouns.

măn	chĭld	fȯe	eow (kou)
wĭfe	frĭend	tûrf	hĕav′ en
hōme	fä′ thēr	eälf	wĕl′ eȯme
house	mȯth′ ẽr	lēaf	kĭn′ drĕd
hănd	sĭs′ tẽr	ăsh′ ĕṣ	fĭre′ sĭde
heärth	brȯth′ ẽr	erä′ dle	neĭgħ′ bor (-bēr)

LESSON CCXXII. Suffixes.

Verbs ending in silent *e* generally drop the *e* when adding *ed* or *ing*. The suffix *ed*, generally, means *did; ing* means *continuing to.*

aeℏed	aeℏ′ ĭng	fōrçed	fōr′ çĭng
ăl lĕged′	ăl lĕg′ ĭng	gāzed	gāz′ ĭng
bê liēved′	bê liēv′ ĭng	griēved	griēv′ ĭng
dīved	dīv′ ĭng	hĕdged	hĕdg′ ĭng
dŏdged	dŏdg′ ĭng	jōked	jōk′ ĭng
ĕx pīred′	ĕx pīr′ ĭng	jŭdged	jŭdg′ ĭng

LESSON CCXXIII. Suffixes, Continued.

lóved	lóv′ ĭng	sāved	sāv′ ĭng
mīned	mīn′ ĭng	seℏēmed	seℏēm′ ĭng
nāmed	nām′ ĭng	sēized	sēiz′ ĭng
piēçed	piēç′ ĭng	skăt′ ĕd	skăt′ ĭng
plāgued	plāgu′ ĭng	squēezed	squēez′ ĭng
rê fūṣed′	rê fūṣ′ ĭng	wăd′ ĕd	wăd′ ĭng

LESSON CCXXIV.

Words frequently mispronounced or improperly accented.

à dŭlt′	bà sạlt′	eŏm′ băt ant
à gain′ (-gĕn′)	brê vĕt′	eŏn′ vēr sant
à lás′	eō′ eôa	eŏm′ plái ṣănt′
à slànt′	eà eā′ ô	dê eā′ dençe
ăs çĕt′ ĭe	eạl′ drón	dĕm′ ŏn strāte
àt tà çhe′ (-shá′)	chās′ ten	ĕx′ quĭ ṣīte lў
à pê′ rĭ ent	çẽre′ mẹnt	ĕx̱′ ĕm plá rў
àr′ eℏĭveṣ	eoûr′ tê oŭs	ê nēr′ vāte
ăd′ vēr tīṣe′	eŏn dŏ′ lençe	gòv′ ẽrn mẹnt
ăth′ lête	çê rụ′ lê an	lăm′ ĕn tà ble
ăm′ à tẽur′	eō′ ăd jū′ tôr	lĕg′ ĕnd à rў

LESSON CCXXV. Synonyms.

These words are to be distinguished carefully from one another.

aid
assist

Aid supposes co-operation on the part of the person who is relieved; *assist* refers to relief given by a person who "stands by" in order to relieve; as, I did all I could to *aid* the man to escape from the burning building; I saw the boy *assist* the old lady to cross the street.

appear
seem

Appear is confined to the senses; *seem* to the mind, as, the man *appears* to be healthy, and *seems* to be contented.

among
amidst

Among denotes a mingling or intermixture; *amidst,* surrounded by; as, "Blessed art thou *among* women;" the book was written *amidst* many interruptions.

allow
permit

We *allow* what we know and silently consent to, or abstain from preventing; we *permit* that to which we give a decided assent; as, the head of a school may *allow* the scholars certain practices for a time which he would not directly *permit.*

avoid
shun

To *avoid* danger is in general not to fall into it; to *shun* it is with care to keep out of the way of it; as, *avoid* quarrels, *shun* bad company.

assent
consent

Assent is an act of the understanding; *consent* of the will or feelings; as, he *assented* to the truth of the statement, and *consented* to act in ac-cordance with it.

admittance
admission

Admittance denotes the permission to enter; *admission,* the actual entry. Thus, we see on the doors of factories, no *admittance,* while we speak of *admission* to the rights of citizenship.

LESSON CCXXVI. Names of great Rivers.

Nïle	Găn' ġēṣ	Mạ dēĭ' rạ	Măe kĕn' zĭe
Rhïne	Kŏṇ' gō	Ăm' ạ zŏn	Căm bō' dị ạ
Lĕ' nạ	Tĭ' grĭs	Zäm bẹ' zĭ	Ä' mur (-mo͞or)
Ĭn' dŭs	Dăn' ŭbe	Lä Plä' tä	Yu' kŏn (Yo͞o' kŏn)
Nĭ' ġẹr	Mŭr' rȧy	Rĕd Rĭv' ēr	Eŭ phrā' (-frā'-) tēṣ
Vŏl' gä	Ō rĭ nō' eŏ	Cŏl' ọ rä' dō	Yăng tsê Kĭ äng'

LESSON CCXXVII. Musical Instruments.

lȳre	eôr' nĕt	zĭth' ēr	flăg' eŏ lĕt
lūte	băn' jŏ	pĭ' ȧ nŏ	eăs' tȧ nĕt
härp	guĭ tär'	fĭd' dle	măn' dô lĭn
flūte	ôr' gan	trŏm' bōne	Jew's' (jūz-) härp
bū' gle	vĭ' ô lĭn'	elăr' ĭ nĕt'	vĭ' ô lŏn çĕl' (-sĕl'-) lŏ

LESSON CCXXVIII. Relating to Music.

kêy	ehôrdṣ	ŭ' nĭ sŏn	quā' (kwā-) vēr
stáff	găm' ŭt	mĕl' ô dy̆	mê lō' dĭ oŭs
seăle	eŏn' çērt	här' mŏ ny̆	sy̆m' phŏ (-fō-) ny̆

LESSON CCXXIX. Flowers.

lĭl' y̆	hy̆' ȧ çĭnth	măg nō' lĭ ȧ
tū' lĭp	bŭt' tēr eŭp'	hŏl' ly̆ hŏck
eăe' tŭs	eŏl' ŭm bĭne	dăn' dê lĭ' ŏn
pŏp' py̆	ȧ zā' lê ȧ	eär na' tion
daĭ' ṣy̆	eȧ mĕl' lĭ ȧ	hê' lĭ ô trōpe
păn' ṣy̆	bê gō' nĭ ȧ	ehry̆s ăn' thê mŭm
pê' ô ny̆	ġê rä' nĭ ŭm	hŏn' ey̆ sŭe' kle
vĭ' ô lĕt	pê tū' nĭ ȧ	ġĕn' tian (-shȧn)
ĕr bê' nȧ	när çĭs' sŭs	däh' liȧ (däl' yȧ)
măr' ĭ gŏld	ȧ nĕm' ô nê	fuçh' sĭ ȧ (fū' shĭ ȧ)
dăf' fô dĭl	glȧ dĭ' ô lŭs	năs tûr' tium (-shŭm)

LESSON CCXXX. Other words used in Geography

rå vīne'	hồ rī' zŏn	bound' å rў
dĕṣ' ērt	Soûth' ērn	ĕs' tû å rў
rāç' ĕṣ	ăn' ĭ måls	Ė qua' tor (-kwâ' tēr)
lå gōōn'	vŏl eā' nồ	phўs' ĭe al (fīz' ĭ kal)
mồ răss'	eồn' tĭ nent	ăv' å lånch
ồ' å sĭs	Ăt lăn' tĭe	år' eħĭ pĕl' å gồ
Nôrth' ērn	moun' taĭn	prồm' ón tồ rў
På çĭf' ĭe	tĕm' pēr åte	pĕn ĭn' sù lå

LESSON CCXXXI. Words used in Drawing.

ĕl līpse'	dī ăg' ồn al	draught (dråft)
rå' dĭ ŭs	lay' fīg' ûre	hồr' ĭ zŏn' tal
păr' al lĕl	dī ăm' ê tēr	sphĕr' ĭe al (sfĕr' ĭ kal)
trī' ăṉ' gle	ĭ sŏs' çê lĕṣ	pēr spĕe' tĭve
măn' ĭ kĭn	ŏb lique' (-lēk')	sўm mĕt' rĭe al
quad' (kwŏd'-) rĭ låt' ēr al		prồ jĕe' tion
ê quĭ (-kwĭ-) låt' ēr al		ĕl' ê vå' tion

LESSON CCXXXII. Words relating to old and new.

fŏs' sĭl	vēr' nal	prĭ mē' val	vĕn' ēr å ble
nŏv' el	mŏd' ērn	ăn çĕs' tral	ăn tique' (tēk')
sê' nĭle	är eħå' ĭe	prĭm' ĭ tĭve	ăn' cient (-shent)
rê' çent	ŏb' sồ lēte	nê ồ tēr' ĭe	prê ăd' am ĭte

LESSON CCXXXIII. Names of some Diseases.

eăn' çēr	jäun' dĭçe	dўs pĕp' sĭ å
drŏp' sў	pleū' rĭ sў	tū' mor (-mēr)
ăb' scĕss	brŏn eħĭ' tĭs	neû rål' gĭ å
ăsth' må	dī ar rħē' å	rheu' må tĭṣm
eå tärrħ'	serŏf' û lå	seår' lĕt fē' vēr
eħŏl' ēr å	hĕm' ồr rħåge	dĭph (dĭf-) thē' rĭ å
mēa' ṣleṣ	på răl' ў sĭs	eồn sŭmp' tion

LESSON CCXXXIV.

The *e* is retained in some words in order to prevent a doubt as to the pronunciation, or to distinguish them from somewhat similar words, as

dȳe′ ĭng	shọe′ ĭng	tĭnġe′ ĭng
hŏe′ ĭng	sĭnġe′ ĭng	tŏe′ ĭng

LESSON CCXXXV.

When the suffix *ed* is added to some regular verbs the *e* is silent while the *d* is pronounced like *t*, as

fīxed (fĭxst)	grāçed (grāst)	erăcked (krăkt)
hĭssed (hĭst)	bŏxed (bŏxst)	serāped (skrāpt)
eŏn fĕssed′ (-fĕst′)		ĕm brāçed′ (-brāst′)
ĕs eāped′ (-kāpt′)		ŏp prĕssed′ (-prĕst′)

LESSON CCXXXVI.

When derivative words formed by adding the suffix *ed* to monosyllables and words accented on the last syllable end in a single consonant preceded by a single vowel, that consonant is doubled. In pronouncing these words the *e* of the suffix is silent, unless preceded by *d* or *t*.

ăe quĭt′ tĕd	fĭt′ tĕd	ŏ mĭt′ tĕd	rŭbbed
eŏm mĭt′ tĕd	frĕt′ tĕd	plănned	shŭnned
eŏm pĕlled′	ĭn fĕrred′	quĭt′ tĕd	tăpped

LESSON CCXXXVII.

When the final consonant of a word is preceded by a diphthong or a digraph representing a vowel sound, or the word ends in two different consonants, or the accent of a word ending in a single consonant falls on any other syllable than the last, the final consonant is not doubled in words of which the suffix begins with a vowel, as:

rāined	daubed	prŏf′ ĭt ĕd	rĕst′ ĕd
ăet′ ĕd	lănd′ ĕd	quar′ rĕled	rĕv′ ĕled
fāiled	mĕr′ ĭt ĕd	pēr fôrmed′	trăv′ ĕled

LESSON CCXXXVIII.
Words hard to spell and their meaning.

ĕt' ĭ quette' (-kĕt) The forms required by polite society.

kĕr' ô sēné   Refined petroleum; coal oil.

sär' sá pá rĭl' lá   A plant.

ŭm brĕl' lá   A folding shade carried in the hand as a protection from the rain or the rays of the sun.

păm' phlĕt (-flĕt) A book made up of a few printed sheets stitched together, but not bound, though sometimes having a paper cover.

sô brī' ê tў   Soberness; temperance.

ĭn dĕl' ĭ ble   That cannot be blotted out; washed away, or removed.

hĕad' aehe   Pain in the head.

ĕm bär' rass   To perplex; hinder; confuse.

à pŏl' ô ġĭze   To make an excuse; to acknowledge a fault and to express regret for it.

ĭm' bê çĭle   Weak; feeble; feeble-minded; idiotic.

fĕm' ĭ nĭne   Relating to women; womanly; tender; delicate.

eòv' ê nant   Agreement; contract; bargain.

bois' tēr oŭs   Loud; noisy; violent; stormy.

frŏn' tĭs pĭēçe The engraving which faces the title page of a book.

ăs sō çĭ ā' tion Union, connection of persons or things; a society; a company.

eū' pô lá   A roof having a rounded form; a dome.

ĭn eūr' à ble   That cannot be cured.

ĭl lŭs' trĭ oŭs Celebrated; distinguished; famous

LESSON CCXXXIX. Synonyms.

These words are to be distinguished carefully from one another.

jealous
envious
    We are *jealous* of what is our own, and fear to lose it; we are *envious* of what another has, and are pained that he has it. Nations are *jealous* of any interference on the part of another power in their commerce, government, or territory; individuals are *envious* of the rank, wealth, and honors of others.

leave
quit
    We *leave* that to which we may intend to return; we *quit* that to which we return no more; we *leave* persons or things; we *quit* things only. I *leave* my house for a short time; I *quit* it not to return to it.

low-priced
cheap
    That for which little has been paid is *low-priced*, though the thing itself may really be dear. *Cheap* is that of which the price is low considering its worth. For example, the watch was very *cheap* though by no means *low-priced*.

malice
spite
    Malice signifies the love of evil for evil's sake; *spite* is a disposition to offend another in trifling matters. Thus, we speak of a deep-seated *malice*, a petty *spite*.

mistake
error
blunder
    A *mistake* is the taking of one thing for another through haste or carelessness; an *error* is a departure from that which is right or correct; a *blunder* signifies anything done blindly, and is a mistake of the grossest kind. We may forgive an *error* and overlook a *mistake*, but a *blunder* is always blamable.

mute
dumb
    One who *can* speak, but for some reason *will not* speak is said to be *mute*. He who *cannot* speak is *dumb*. For example, he was *mute* in spite of all threats; the boy was born deaf and *dumb*.

LESSON CCXL. Words often Confounded.

rĕl'ĭe, anything preserved in remembrance.

rĕl' ĭet, a widow.

rout, to defeat, to beat.

route, the way which is traveled.

răd' ĭsh, an edible root.

rĕd' dĭsh, somewhat red.

sē' rĭ oŭs, grave; solemn.

Sĭr' ĭ ŭs, the *Dog-star*.

sēize, to catch; capture.

çēase, to stop.

stăt' ŭe, a carved image.

stăt' ūte, law; regulation; decree.

sĕn' trў, guard; watch.

çĕnt' ŭ rў, a period of a hundred years.

stałk, the stem of a plant.

stŏck, supply; capital; the race of a family.

săt, did sit.

sĭt, to rest, as on a chair; to fit.

sĕt, to fix; to place on; to appoint.

LESSON CCXLI. Dictation Exercise.

There is a relic of St. Peter and his bronze statue in Rome. Jacob married the relict of Eli. There is a new route to Florida. The radish adds flavor to a meal. The lady's gown is of a reddish hue. The enemy tried to seize the post, but the sentry was able to rout them though he received a serious wound. The rising of Sirius and of the sun in the same part of the heavens used to be considered as the cause of the summer's heat. The statute against forgery is more than a century old. Unless you cease your dissipation, your stock of merchandize will be used up. The stalk of the rose-bush is broken. I told the porter to set the vase on the table and then sit down; he sat down.

LESSON CCXLII. Latin Roots.

ago, actum = *to do, to perform;* **amo** = *to love;* **annus** — *the year.*

1. a′ ġĕnt	7. ăg′ Ĭ tāte	13. ăm′ Ĭ eȧ ble
2. ăe′ tĭve	8. ă ġĭl′ Ĭ tў	14. Ĭn Ĭm′ Ĭ eal
3. dăm′ ȧġe	9. ăm′ ȯr oŭs	15. ăn′ naḻṣ
4. ăe′tû ate	10. a′ mĭ ȧ ble	16. ăn′ nȗ al
5. ĕn ăet′	11. ĕn′ ė mў	17. ăn nū′ Ĭ tў
6. trăns ăet′	12. ăm′ ȧ teṵr′	18. çĕn′ tê nȧ rў

19. ăn nĬ vĕr′ sȧ rў   20. pĕr ĕn′ nĬ al

DEFINITION. 1 means one who is authorized to act for another. 2, busy. 3, hurt, injury. 4, to put into action. 5, to establish by law. 6, to do, to perform. 7, to shake. 8, activity. 9, loving. 10, worthy to be loved. 11, one who hates. 12, one who is attached to any particular study or art. 13, friendly. 14, unfriendly. 15, record of events, each under the year in which it happened. 16, yearly. 17, a yearly allowance. 18, occurring once in a hundred years. 19, the yearly return of the day on which an event happened. 20, continual.

LESSON CCXLIII. Latin Roots.

audio, auditum = *to hear;* **animus** = *the mind;* **aqua** = *water;*
æquus = *equal.*

The *qu* of many of the following words is pronounced as if spelled *kw.*

1. aṵ′ dĬt	7. Ĭn ăn′ Ĭ mȧte	13. ė′ qual Ĭze
2. aṵ′ dĬ ble	8. û năn′ Ĭ moŭs	14. ė quȧl′ Ĭ tў
3. aṵ′ dĬ ençe	9. ē quȧ nĭm′ Ĭ tў	15. ė quā′ tŏr
4. aṵ′ dĬ tô rў	10. ȧ quăt′ Ĭe	16. ė′ quĬ nȯx
5. ăn′ Ĭ mā′ tion	11. ăq′ uė dŭet	17. ĕq′ uĬ tў
6. ăn′ Ĭ mŏs′ Ĭ tў	12. ȧ quā′ rĬ ŭm	18. ė′ quȧ ble

19. ăd′ ė quáte   20. Ĭn Ĭq′ uĬ tў

DEFINITION. 1 means to examine and adjust, as an account. 2, loud enough to be heard. 3, an assembly of hearers. 4, of or pertaining to hearing. 5, liveliness. 6, hatred. 7, lifeless. 8, being of one mind. 9, calmness. 10, pertaining to water. 11, an artificial passage for conducting water. 12, a globe or tank in which live fishes and aquatic plants are kept. 13, to make equal. 14, the quality of being equal. 15, the imaginary circle on the earth's surface. 16, the time of the year when the sun enters one of the points near the equator. 17, natural right. 18, equal and uniform. 19, fully sufficient. 20, wickedness.

LESSON CCXLIV.

Words frequently mispronounced or improperly accented.

Ăl' dĭne	dŏl' ôr oŭs	hŏ mê ŏp' å thў
ăs pĭr' ant	dĭs çĭ' ple	ĭn' tēr ĕst ĭng
ăb dŏ' mĕn	ê lĕ' g̣ĭ ăe	ĭm' bê çĭle
å rŏ' må	ĕq' uĭ pȧg̣e	ĭm' pȯ tent
ŭe elĭ' mâte	ĕx̱ ĕe' û tôr	mĭs' chĭê voŭs
brĭg' and	Eῠ rȯ pē' an	mû ṣē' ŭm
bĕn' zĭne	ĕx' pŭr gȧte	ôr' thȯ ê pў
çў'nȯ sụre (-shụr)	fŏre' hĕad	prê çĕd' ençe
eŏg nŏ' mĕn	fŭl' sȯme	prê eŏ' cioŭs (-shŭs)
eŏṇ' eôrd	fĕm' ĭ nĭne	sŭb' lû nå rў
dĕf' ĭ çĭt	g̣ĕn' û ĭne	trê mĕn' doŭs

LESSON CCXLV.

The suffixes *ar*, *er*, *or*, added to a noun mean *one who*, or *that which*, as *runner*, one who runs, *clipper*, that which clips. To words ending in *e*, *r* only is added.

ăd vĭṣ' ēr	elĭp' pēr	law' yēr	rĕad' ēr
bĕg' gar (-ēr)	dĭg' gēr	moụrn' ēr	rŭb' bēr
bê lĭev' ēr	drŭm' mēr	ŏwn' ēr	sûr vĭv' or (-ēr)
bŏast' ēr	ĕn grāv' ēr	pāv' ēr	swĭm' mēr
buĭld' ēr	gĭv' ēr	plănt' ēr	wrĕs' tlēr

LESSON CCXLVI.

The suffix *er* added to an adjective means *more*.

brĭght' ēr	glăd' dēr	loōs' ēr	shôrt' ēr
broạd' ēr	grĭm' mēr	măd' dēr	slĭght' ēr
eōld' ēr	hănd' sọm ēr	prĕt' (prĭt') tĭ ēr	smoōth' ēr
därk' ēr	här' dēr	rĭp' ēr	thĭn' nēr
dĭm' mēr	hĕav' ĭ ēr	roŭgh' (rŭf-') ēr	yoŭṇ' gēr

LESSON CCXLVII. Homonyms.

stĕel, a composition of iron.

stăre, to gaze at.

stĕal, to take without right.

stâir, a series of steps.

stȳle, diction; manner.

sûr'plŭs, more than is needed.

stĭle, steps over a fence or wall.

sûr'plĭçe, the white gar-ment worn by a priest over his cassock.

sōar, to fly aloft.

târe, allowance in weight.

sōre, a place where the skin and flesh are brok-en or bruised.

teâr, to pull apart.

thrōne, a chair of state.

thrōwn, cast.

sŭm, amount of two or more numbers added.

tǫ, unto; towards.

too, more than enough.

sóme, a little; a part.

twǫ, one and one.

LESSON CCXLVIII. Dictation Exercise.

Steel frames are now used for many buildings. There is more honor in being raised to a throne than in being born to one. Four is the sum of two and two. While trying to steal the thief received a blow which knocked him down the stair. If you have too much money give the surplus to some charity. The tare on the case was twenty pounds. Goldsmith's writings are a model of style. The higher we soar the greater the fall. In taking the surplice out of the drawer the acolyte was so un-fortunate as to tear it. The girl who tried to stare at the sun has now a sore eye. In crossing the stile my aunt tripped, and was thrown down.

LESSON CCXLIX.
Words in which *a* is often Mispronounced.

fär	eá*t*ch	da′ tá	ạl′ wáyş
yẹa	dráin	lä′ vá	eá nä′ rў
ฅä*l*m	groạt	mä′ ġĭ	ĕm bä*l*m′
färm	hä*l*ve	áft′ ẽr	pá shä′
ฅănt	sháft	daí′ rў	á g*h*ást′
eán′t	glánçe	lánçe	bá nä′ná

LESSON CCL.

The suffixes *yer, ier, eer, ist,* and *ian* signify *one who practices* or *belongs to* a certain profession.

sạw′ yẽr	voy′ á ġẽr	ärt′ ĭst	bŏt′ án ĭst
eăsh *i*ẽr′	ĕn′ ġĭ nẹẹr′	drŭg′ gĭst	sōl′ diẽr (-jẽr)
fûr′ rĭ ẽr	ạwẹ′ tion ẽẹr′	plán′ ĭst	grăm mä′ rĭ ăn

LESSON CCLI.
Some more words in which *a* is often Mispronounced.

lä′ má	hä′ rĕm	seârçe	păg′ eant
pá pä′	jäl′ ạp	tránçe	seăth′ lĕss
ạl′ dẽr	sạu′ çẽr	tär′ Iff	fạl′ chion (-chŭn)
á máss′	hĭ ä′ tŭs	stămp	chăl′ drón
eá′ rĕt	bä′ thŏs	pạu′ pẽr	hạl′ bẽrd
fáir′ ў	eä′ rĭ oŭs	mám mä	băr′ rĭ eáde′

LESSON CCLII. Studies.

Grẹẹk	shôrt′ hănd	tўpe′ wrĭt′ ĭng
Lăt′ ĭn	ġê ŏm′ ê trў	lĭt′ ẽr á tûre
Frĕnch	ás trŏn′ ô mў	bŏŏk′ kẹep′ ĭng
Spán′ ĭsh	Ĭ täl′ ian (-yạn)	grăm′ mar (-mẽr)
hў′ ġĭ ēne	r*h*ĕt′ ô rĭe	măth′ ê măt′ ĭes
Ġẽr′ man	e*h*ĕm′ ĭs trў	pĕn′ man shĭp
stê nŏg′ rá phў (-fў)	phўs (fĭs-) ĭ ŏl′ ô ġў

LESSON CCLIII. Synonyms.

These words are to be distinguished carefully from one another.

paint
dye
To *paint* is to cover or smear over with color ; to *dye* is to dip in any color. For example, we *paint* a house, a barn, a carriage. We *dye* our clothes.

revenge
avenge
To *revenge* is to inflict pain or injury for injury done to ourselves or others ; to *avenge* is to · inflict just punishment in behalf of ourselves or of others. Thus, we *avenge* our wrongs; God will *avenge* the wrongs of the oppressed ; out of *revenge* for a fancied wrong the soldier shot his captain.

request
ask
beg
To *request* is a polite way of asking ; as, we *request* the pleasure of a friend's company to dinner. To *ask* is the general term to denote an expression of our wishes for what we want from another; as, we *ask* what time it is. To *beg*, in its original sense was to *ask* with earnestness, and carried with it the idea of submission: as, to *beg* for food. It has now taken the place of *ask* and *request* on the ground of its expressing more of deference and request: thus, we *beg* a friend to accept a present: a tradesman *begs* to call attention to his new stock of goods.

rest
repose
Rest is a ceasing from motion or labor; *repose* is that kind of rest which gives relief and refreshment after work. *Repose* is a necessity: the weary seek *repose*. We may *rest* while standing: to *repose* we must lie down.

retirement
solitude
seclusion
Retirement is the act of withdrawing from society or from public life; *solitude* is the state of being alone; *seclusion* describes the fact that a person is shut out from others, usually by his own choice.

LESSON CCLIV.

Other words in which *a* is often mispronounced

slånt	swăthe	prai' rĭe	squä' (skwä'-) lŏr
străp	seâred	lĭt ēr ă' tĭm	ăn' cient (-shent)
seăth	răft' ēr	ăf flä' tŭs	gua' (gwä'-) nô
tä' pĭs	făr ra' gô	seạl' lóp	quag' (kwăg'-) mĭre
rä' dĭx	eråft' ў̆	ả' prĭ eŏt	à qua' (-kwä'-) rĭ ŭm

LESSON CCLV.

Some more words in which *a* is often mispronounced.

pä' rĭ àh	săe' rà ment	ĕx pä' trĭ ăte
ŏe tä' vô	văl' en tĭne	ŭl tĭ ma' tŭm
pạl' freў̆	frä' tēr nĭze	eŏm mảnd' ment
mäel' strôm	măn dä' mŭs	g̈ў̆m nä' ṣĭ ŭm
är eä' nŭm	grả vä' mĕn	zouave (zwäv)

LESSON CCLVI.

The suffixes *dom, hood, ness,* and *ship* mean *state of being, character, condition,* and *office.*

wĭṣ' dóm	Chrĭs' ten dóm	ĭll' nĕss
frēe' dóm	môth' ēr hŏŏd	săd' nĕss
sērf' dóm	mäid' en hŏŏd	fụll' nĕss
kĭng' dóm	eōarse' nĕss	dĕaf' nĕss
ēarl' dóm	toŭgh' (tŭf-) nĕss	kĭnd' nĕss
thrạll' dóm	lä' zĭ nĕss	lēan' nĕss
mär' tўr dóm	wēa' rĭ nĕss	mēan' nĕss
fạlse' hŏŏd	sạu' çĭ nĕss	elōse' nĕss
knĭght' hŏŏd	weight' ĭ nĕss	sweet' nĕss
här' dĭ hŏŏd	drow' ṣĭ nĕss	numb' nĕss
lĭke' lĭ hŏŏd	elĕan' lĭ nĕss	frĭend' shĭp
wĭd' ôw hŏŏd	bus' (bĭz-) i nĕṣs	lôrd' shĭp
lĭve' li hŏŏd	eóme (kŭm-) lĭ nĕss	rê lä' tion shĭp

LESSON CCLVII. Latin Roots.

cado, casum = *to fall;* **capio, captum** = *to take;* **dico,**
dictum = *to say.*

1. dĕ eā́ý	7. ĕx çĕpt́	13. rĕḉ Ĭ pê
2. eăs´(kăzh-´) û al	8. dĕ çĕ́ivé	14. vēr´ dĭet
3. eā́ dençe	9. rĕ çĕ́ipt́	15. dĭe´ tion
4. ăe´ çĭ dent	10. eăp´ tĭve	16. dĭe´ tăte
5. eŏ́ Ĭn çĭde´	11. ŏe´ eû pȳ	17. ăd dĭet´
6. ŏe eā́ sion (-zhŭn)	12. eŏn çĕit´	18. ĕ´ dĭet

DEFINITION. 1 means to rot. 2, accidental. 3, a fall of the voice
in reading or speaking. 4, a sudden and unexpected event. 5, to cor-
respond exactly. 6, a convenient chance. 7. to omit. 8, to mislead.
9, an acknowledgment of money paid. 10, a prisoner taken by force.
11, to hold or keep for use. 12, vanity. 13, a formulary for making some
mixture. 14, a decision. 15, language. 16, to command. 17, to apply
habitually. 18, a command, a proclamation.

LESSON CCLVIII. Latin Roots.

dignus = *worthy;* **duco, ductum** = *to lead;* **facio,**
factum = *to make.*

1. de̩ign	7. eŏn´ dŭet	13. ăb dŭe´ tion
2. eŏn dĭgn´	8. rĕ dūçé	14. vĭ́ à dŭet
3. dĭs dāin´	9. dŭe´ tĭle	15. ăf fĕet´
4. dĭg´ nĭ tȳ	10. Ĭn dūçé	16. făe´ tŏ rȳ
5. dĭg´ nĭ fȳ	11. prŏd´ ŭet	17. pēr´ fĕet
6. Ĭn dĭg´ nant	12. ĕd´ ŭ eāte	18. făe´ ŭl tȳ

19. dĕ fĭ´ cient (-fĭsh´ ent)   20. săe´ rĭ fice (-fĭz)

DEFINITION. 1 means to condescend to give. 2, deserved. 3, to
think unworthy. 4, true worth, excellence. 5, to honor. 6, affected with
anger mingled with contempt. 7, behavior, management. 8, to diminish,
to lessen. 9, easily led. 10, to move, to influence. 11, result, fruit,
effect. 12, to teach, to train. 13, a carrying away. 14, a bridge; a
structure for carrying a road, as a railroad. 15, to influence. 16, the
place where workmen are employed in making goods. 17, finished,
faultless. 18, talent, ability. 19, imperfect. 20, the offering of any thing
to God; the surrender of any thing for the sake of some one or something
else.

LESSON CCLIX. Homonyms.

plăin, simple; even; flat.

plăne, a tool for smoothing wood or metal.

pĕer, an equal.

pĭĕr, a wharf or landing place.

răp, to knock on.

wrăp, to wind or fold together; to envelope completely,

rŏde, did ride.

rŏad, street; passage.

rŏwed, did row.

străĭt, narrow.

străĭght, not crooked.

sŏle, the bottom of the foot.

sŏul, the spiritual part in man.

săĭl' ĕr, with a qualifying word descriptive of the manner of sailing; a ship or other vessel.

săĭl' or (-ĕr), a seaman.

sŭn, the heavenly body which gives the light of day.

sŏn, a male child.

LESSON CCLX. Dictation Exercise.

Let the pupils fill out the blanks with the missing words.

Gladstone, though only plain Mister is the —— of any man in England. The old ship is such a very slow sailer that she has only just arrived at her ——. While my son was crossing the room he struck the —— of his foot against a plane. The road alongside the cliff is very strait. At midday the —— is very hot. When the sailor rowed us out to the ship the wind was so cold I had to —— my cloak around me. Your boy ought not enter the room without first stopping to —— at the door. My uncle always sat straight when he —— on horseback. To gain the whole world is nothing if you lose your ——.

LESSON CCLXI. Words hard to spell and their meaning.

rĭ dĭe′ ŭ loŭs	Absurd and laughable.
săn̯′ guine (-gwĭn)	Warm; lively; hopeful.
prŏph′ (prŏf′-) ĕ sy̆	To tell of things to come.
ẹăl′ ŭm ny̆	A false accusation made with malice.
bă̯y′ ô nĕt	A short sword or dagger fitted to a musket or rifle.
lĭn′ ĕ âġe	Descendants in a direct line.
môrt′ găġe	A conditional conveyance of property, as security for a debt.
jŏe′ ŭ lar (-lẽr)	Given to jesting.
vouch sāfe′	Condescend to grant.
är′ eℏĭveṣ	Public records preserved as evidence of facts.
dĭ lĕm′ mả	A difficult or doubtful choice.
ĕ′ lăs tĭç′ ĭ ty̆	Springiness; tendency to rebound.
tŏl′ ẽr ả ble	That may be borne or endured.
ŏp′ tion	Left to one's own choice.
na̯ugh′ ty̆	Guilty of improper conduct.
ha̯ugh′ ty̆	Proud and contemptuous.
fĭ′ ẽr y̆	Passionate; very active.
gℏâst′ ly̆	Pale; deathlike.
hĭe′ eough (-kŭp)	A convulsive sob or cough.
vĭct′ uảlṣ	Food for human beings.
zeph′ yr (zĕf′ ẽr)	The west wind; any mild, soft wind.
wrĕtch′ ĕd	Unhappy; worthless.
ŭn′ ion (-yŭn)	The uniting or joining of two or more things into one.
ô bĭt′ ŭ ả ry̆	An account of a deceased person.
çhăm′ oiṣ (-my̆)	A kind of antelope; a soft leather.

LESSON CCLXII.

Words frequently mispronounced or improperly accented

sạu' çў	těn' à ble	ăl' mŏnd
swạth	těp' ĭd	Ăr' ăb
săt' ĭre	tï' nў	a' rê à
sä' tўr	tŏn tïne'	Ăl' pĭne
stĭr' rŭp	trĭb' ūne	bê trŏth'
sŭb' tïle	tê lĕg' rà phў	eạlk
sĭm' ô nў	và gä' rў	eŏn' trà rў
sŭp' ple	vē' hê ment	eŏn' tù mê lў
sўr' ĭnġe	vï' rïle	eŏn dŏ' lençe
sô nŏ' roŭs	vŏl' à tïle	dĭ lāte'
soŏt	vĭe' ar (-ēr)	dĭs' pù tant
tăs' sel	vāse	ĕn' ġĭne
tô mä' tô	věn' ĭ ŝon	ĕx těm' pô rê

LESSON CCLXIII.

The termination *full* means *filled* with something, as, *woeful*, filled with *woe*. The final *l* is omitted in the derivatives.

ạw' fụl	skĭll' fụl	pēaçe' fụl	dū'tĭ fụl
ärt' fụl	spĭte' fụl	wräth' fụl	pĭt' ĭ fụl
joy' fụl	mŏurn' fụl	frĭght' fụl	făn' çĭ fụl
wĭll' fụl	grāçe' fụl	chănġe' fụl	boun' tĭ fụl

LESSON CCLXIV.

The suffixes *en, ish, y,* and *some* mean *having the quality of.*

hĕmp' en	wăx' en	dŭst' ў	lŏath' sòme
brä' zen	jūĭ' çў	hŏg'gĭsh	blīthe' sòme
lĕad' en	rŏck' ў	fĭend' ĭsh	mĕd' dle sòme
ĕarth' en	sĭl' vĕr ў	knäv' ĭsh	troŭb' le sòme
ĕn lĭv' en	sä'vor(-vĕr-)ў	shrew' ĭsh	věn' tûre sòme
bēech' en	sĭn' ew ў	wĭn' sòme	wēa' rĭ sòme
ĕm bŏld'en	stŏn' ў	toil' sòme	eŭm' bêr sòme

LESSON CCLXV. Synonyms.

These words are to be distinguished carefully from one another.

amaze
astonish
What we cannot understand may *amaze* us; what is great or very striking is apt to *astonish* us.

apology
excuse
We make an *apology* for unbecoming conduct; we offer an *excuse* for neglect of duty. For example: The teacher accepted the boy's *excuse*, but made him offer an *apology* for what he had done.

apparent
evident
obvious
That which appears to the eye or is already seen is *apparent;* that which is seen or clearly proved is *evident;* while that which proves itself or is readily perceived is *obvious.*

aged
elderly
old
Aged and *elderly* are more commonly applied to persons; *old* to persons or things; as, an *elderly* couple; an *aged* man lives in that *old* house.

accurate
exact
precise
A thing is *accurate* when done in *careful* conformity to the right; it is *exact* when brought to that perfect state in which there is no defect, and it is *precise* when it strictly conforms to some rule or model, as if *cut down* thereto ; as, an *accurate* account, an *exact* measure, *precise* language.

authentic
genuine
A book is *authentic* when it relates matters of fact as they really happened: it is *genuine* when it is written by the person whose name it bears. A book may be *genuine* without being *authentic,* or it may be *authentic* without being *genuine.*

ability
capacity
Ability is the power of doing something; *capacity* is the power of receiving something, as, for instance, new ideas, etc. *Capacity* is needed to plan, *ability* to carry out a great enterprise. We speak of the *ability* with which a book is written, or an argument is maintained. Some lawyers have *capacity* to excel in their profession.

LESSON CCLXVI. Homonyms.

mā*i*n, strength.

mān*e*, the long hair on the neck of a horse, lion, etc.

mē*e*t, fit; proper.

mē*a*t, food in general.

nō*ş*e, the part of the face which is the organ of smell.

*k*nō*w*ş, understands.

our, belonging to us.

*h*our, sixty minutes.

pān*e*, one of the pieces of glass in a door or sash.

pā*i*n, suffering.

ō*a*r, an instrument for rowing boats.

ō*r*e, metal as taken from the mine.

ō'*er*, a contraction for *over*.

p*a*w*ş*, the feet of certain animals.

p*a*u*ş*e, to stop; to wait.

r*e*ẽ*i*n, an instrument for curbing or governing.

r*e*ẽ*ig*n, to govern; to rule.

rā*i*n, water falling in drops from the air.

LESSON CCLXVII. Dictation Exercise.

My father caught the runaway horse by the mane, and held it till the rein was mended. The girl has a pain in her nose, but she works with might and main. It is meet to give every one his due. I have a piece of ore. Pray that our Holy Father may live to reign many years. There is more in the meat than in the carving. The oar is in the boat. The dog's paws are muddy; he knows his master. I hear the rain against the window pane. *O'er* is used for *over* only in poetry. The clock is striking the hour. Pause when tempted to do wrong.

LESSON CCLXVIII.

Words hard to spell and their meaning.

ăe′ qui (-kwĭ-) ĕsce′ To remain satisfied with.

bănk′ rŭpt çӯ Failure or inability to pay debts.

erӯs′ tal līze To cause to form crystals.

ŏe′ stá sӯ Excessive joy; a state in which the body seems as if dead and the senses are suspended, but the soul, retaining full power, is absorbed in God.

ŏf′ fĕr vĕsce′ To bubble and hiss as fluids do when some part escapes in the form of gas.

ê rā′ sure (-zhûr) A scratching out.

făl′ lĭ bĭl′ ĭ tӯ Liability to deceive or to be deceived.

griĕv′ oŭs Causing grief or sorrow.

há răngue′ To make a public speech.

ĭn çĭp′ ĭ ent Beginning.

jĕop′ ard (-ĕrd) ӯ Exposure to death or injury; danger.

knŭe′ kle A joint of the finger.

lĕth′ ár ġӯ A deep, unnatural sleep from which it is difficult to awaken a person.

lăb′ ӯ rĭnth Any inclosure full of difficult turnings.

mĭ răe′ û loŭs Performed by supernatural power.

neû′ tral īze To destroy the peculiar properties of.

ôr′ thŏ dŏx Sound in opinion or doctrine.

pá rō′ ehĭ al Belonging to a parish.

quo (kwŏ-) tā′ tion A part of a book or writing named, repeated, or brought forward as evidence or illustration.

rĕt′ ĭ çĕnçe The state of keeping silence.

slaugh′ tĕr Bloody destruction of life.

û nique′ (-nēk′) Being without a like or equal.

LESSON CCLXIX. Latin Roots.

fero, latum = *to bear;* **finis** = *end;* **fluo, fluxum** = *to flow.*

1. fĕr′ rў	7. prĕf′ ēr ençe	13. dĕf′ ĭ nĭte
2. ê lāte′	8. trăns lā′ tion	14. ăf fĭn′ ĭ tў
3. dĭf′ fēr	9. fī′ nal	15. flū′ ĭd
4. sŭf′ fēr	10. fĭn′ ĭsh	16. flū′ en çў
5. prĕl′ âte	11. eŏn fīne′	17. flŭe′ tû âte
6. eŏl lāte′	12. ĭn′ fĭn ĭte	18. ăf′ flû ençe

19. ĭn′ flû ençe   20. sū pēr′ flû oŭs

DEFINITION. 1 means a place where persons or things are carried across a river. 2, to raise the spirit of. 3, to disagree in opinion. 4, to feel or undergo pain. 5, a clergyman having authority over the lower clergy. 6, to compare critically; to gather and place in order. 7, choice. 8, removal; the act of rendering into another language. 9, last. 10, to put an end to. 11, to bound, inclose, imprison. 12, endless. 13, certain, fixed. 14, relation, resemblance. 15, liquid. 16, smoothness; readiness of utterance. 17, to waver, to be unsteady. 18, plenty. 19, power, authority. 20, unnecessary, excessive.

LESSON CCLXX. Latin Roots.

gratus = *thankful;* **gravis** = *heavy;* **habeo, habitum,** = *to have, to hold.*

1. grāçe	7. dĭs grāçe′	13. grăv′ ĭ tāte
2. grāte′ ful	8. eŏn grăt′ û lāte	14. ăg′ grȧ văte
3. grēet	9. griēf	15. hăb′ ĭt
4. grăt′ ĭ fў	10. grāve	16. ex hĭb′ ĭt
5. grȧ tū′ ĭ tў	11. griĕv′ oŭs	17. hȧ bĭt′ û al
6. grăt′ ĭ tūde	12. grăv′ ĭ tў	18. prȯ hĭb′ ĭt

19. hăb ĭ tā′ tion   20. dė bĭl′ ĭ tāte

DEFINITION. 1 means mercy, favor; elegance; the mercy of God. 2, thankful, pleasing. 3, to salute, to welcome, to address with friendship. 4, to please. 5, a free gift; a present. 6, thankfulness. 7, shame, dishonor. 8, to wish joy to. 9, sorrow. 10, solemn, serious. 11, causing sorrow. 12, sobriety of character. 13, to tend toward any object. 14, to provoke, to magnify. 15, manner. 16, to show in order to attract notice. 17, usual, common. 18, to forbid. 19, settled dwelling, residence. 20, to weaken, to enfeeble.

LESSON CCLXXI.

The suffix *age* means *the state* or *quality of being* or *place.*

dŏ' tȧġe	pēr' sȯn ȧġe	ĕs' pȋ ȯ nȧġe
bŏnd' ȧġe	păt' rȯn ȧġe	măr' rȧġe
hērb' ȧġe	hēr' mȋt ȧġe	pȋl' grȋm ȧġe
whȧrf' ȧġe	pū' pȋl ȧġe	vēr' bȋ ȧġe
fĕr' rȋ ȧġe	văs' sal ȧġe	văg' ȧ bŏnd' ȧġe

LESSON CCLXXII.

The suffixes *al, ile, ic, ary,* and *ory* signify *relating to.*

lŏg' ĭe	eûr' sȯ rў	plăn' ĕt ȧ rў	eŭs' tȯm ȧ rў
pȯ ĕt' ĭe	lȋt' ēr ȧ rў	ȋn dŭs' trȋ ăl	prė păr' ȧ tȯ rў
răd' ĭ eăl	jū' vė nȋle	mė dȋç' ȋ năl	ȋn' trȯ dūe' tȯ rў
ŏp' tĭe ăl	eăp' ȋl lȧr ў	trȋb' û tȧ rў	măn' dȧ tȯ rў
eȯm' ĭe ăl	ȋn' fan tȋle	mēr' eăn tȋle	săt' ȋs făe' tȯ rў

LESSON CCLXXIII.

Ly means *like,* of which it is an abbreviation. It is sometimes shortened into *y.*

sȋŋ' glў	seârçe' lў	hĕav' ȋ lў	fōōl' ȋsh lў
foul' lў	hŭm' blў	slēep' ȋ lў	fôr' mēr lў
ĕas' ȋ lў	fōurth' lў	rĕad' ȋ lў	fôrm' ăl lў
doŭb' lў	hăs' tȋ lў	tĕr' rȋ blў	stĕad' ȋ lў
hărsh' lў	nois' ȋ lў	mȋght' ȋ lў	spēed' ȋ lў
whȯl' lў	glōōm' ȋ lў	strănġe' lў	prŏb' ȧ blў
blȋthe' lў	plăin' lў	friĕnd' lў	pĕaçe' fṳl lў

LESSON CCLXXIV.

The suffix *ise* or *ize* means *to make.*

rĕ' al ȋze	ē' qual ȋze	au' thŏr ȋze	năt' û ral ȋze
çȋv' ȋ lȋze	erȋt' ȋ çȋse	hū' man ȋze	ġĕn' ēr al ȋze
û' tȋl ȋze	eăt' ė eḥȋse	sĕe' û lȧr ȋze	Ҁhrȋs' tian ȋze

LESSON CCLXXV. Synonyms.

These words are to be distinguished carefully from one another.

casual
accidental
incidental

A thing is *casual* when it happens by chance, without being prearranged; it is *accidental* when opposed to what is designed, planned, or foreseen; it is *incidental* when it falls *into* some regular course of things, but forms no necessary part thereof; as, a *casual* encounter, a *casual* remark; an *accidental* circumstance; an *accidental* meeting; an *incidental* observation.

custom
habit

Custom is the frequent repetition of the same act; *habit* is the effect of such repetition. *Custom* supposes an act of the will; *habit* is a kind of "second nature", which grows up within us; as, an old *custom;* a fixed *habit.*

celebrate
commemorate

To *celebrate* is to distinguish by some expression of honor and joy; to *commemorate* is to keep in memory by some public solemn ceremony; as, we *celebrate* the birthday of our country's Independence by the observance of the Fourth of July; Christians *commemorate* the death of our Saviour on Good Friday.

confess
acknowledge

We *confess* what we feel to have been wrong; we *acknowledge* what we feel must and ought to be known; a prisoner *confesses* his crime and is punished; a gentleman *acknowledges* his mistakes.

content
satisfy

To *content* is to appease, even though every desire or appetite is not gratified; to *satisfy* is to gratify fully the longings of desire, as, a man who is poor but *content* is rich though all his needs are not *satisfied.*

LESSON CCLXXVI.
Difficult words found in a Second Reader.
Let the pupils write these words.

threw	sought	sheaves	weather
rough	least	months	minute
lose	wolves	plague	women
whole	thieves	warmth	ocean
worms	stalks	steady	carriage

LESSON CCLXXVII. Difficult words from a Second Reader.
To be written by the pupils.

victuals	soldier	telegraph	orchard
sergeant	ironing	squirrel	imagine
courage	angler	stretched	besieged
naughty	venture	buried	whistling
pleasure	choir	question	thrashed
certainly	knock	business	daughter

LESSON CCLXXVIII. Difficult words from a Second Reader.
To be written by the pupils.

column	sacristy	themselves	guardian
anxious	vegetables	lightning	gratitude
quinces	crucified	excellent	delicate
medicine	exception	resembles	collections
triumph	staggered	delightful	affectionate

LESSON CCLXXIX. Difficult words found in a Third Reader.
To be written by the pupils.

poultry	perched	sociable	quantities
machine	doubled	worthless	familiar
gambols	majesty	perceived	complained
suitable	appetites	weighing	imagination
spheres	bustled	palatable	immediately

LESSON CCLXXX. Punctuation.

The **Period** (.) should be used,—

At the end of every complete sentence which does not ask a question or express emotion; as,

It is a beautiful sight to see the sun rise.

After every abbreviated word; as,—

Gen. Geo. Washington. The Rt. Rev. Bishop.

The **Comma** (,) is used,—

To separate two words in a series in the same construction if used without one of the conjunctions *and*, *or*, *nor;* as,

The brief, haughty, gratification of revenge is often purchased at the cost of a lasting, humiliating remorse.

To separate *three* or *more* nouns, adjectives, verbs, participles or adverbs, with or without a conjunction, and also the last word, if it be a *noun*, from the verb; as,

Love, honor, and obey God.
We must not only pity, but also help, the poor.

To separate successive pairs of words joined by a conjunction; as,

Whether we eat or drink, labor or sleep, we should be moderate.

To separate contrasted words or words in opposition; as,

Though deep, yet clear.

Before and after a qualifying clause introduced by a relative; as,

Peace at any price, which these men advocate, means war at any cost.

LESSON CCLXXXI. Punctuation.

The Comma, continued.

To separate the rest of the sentence from parenthetical expressions; as,

The book was oblong, ten inches in length and seven in breadth, and bound in morocco.

To separate from the rest of the sentence a word or an expression denoting a person or an object addressed; as,

Friends, Romans, and countrymen, lend me your ears.

After a nominative, where the verb is understood; as,

To err is human; to forgive, divine.

To separate words and phrases in apposition; as,

Paul, the apostle of the Gentiles, was eminent for his zeal and knowledge.

Between the transposed parts when a sentence is placed out of its natural order; as,

In all pursuits, attention is of primary importance.

After the adverbs *nay, however, finally, at least,* etc.; as,

However, they had not gone far, when they came to a sign post.

After the words *as, namely,* and *to wit,* when introducing an example; as,

There were only three persons in the room; namely, the prisoner, the witness, and the judge.

The Note of Exclamation (!) must be used,—

After every word or phrase which expresses passion or emotion; as,

Dear me! Alas!

LESSON CCLXXXII. Latin Roots.

mater = *mother;* **pater** = *father;* **frater** = *brother;* **homo** = *man.*

1. mă′ tròn	7. pă′ tròn	13. frá tēr′ nal
2. mà tēr′ nal	8. păt′ ròn Ize	14. hū′ man
3. măt′ rĭ mò nў	9. pà tēr′ nal	15. hŏm′ ăge
4. mà tēr′ nĭ tў	10. pà tēr′ nĭ tў	16. hû māne′
5. măt′ rĭ çĭde	11. păt′ rĭ mò nў	17. hū′ man Ize
6. mà trĭe′ û lāte	12. frĭ′ ar (-ēr)	18. hŏm′ ĭ çĭde

DEFINITION. 1 means a wife or a widow. 2, motherly. 3, a sacrament which gives grace to the husband and wife to live happily together. 4, the character or relation of a mother. 5, the murder of a mother by her child. 6, to enter or admit to membership in a society or other body. 7, one who protects. 8, to favor. 9, fatherly. 10, family headship, fatherhood. 11, an estate inherited from one's father. 12, a member of a mendicant religious Order. 13, brotherly. 14, having the qualities or attributes of a man. 15, respect. 16, benevolent. 17, to make gentle, to refine. 18, the killing of one human being by another.

LESSON CCLXXXIII. Latin Roots.

mitto, missum = *to send;* **loquor, locutus** = *to speak;*
manus = *the hand;* **lego, lectum** = *to read.*

1. mĭs′ sion	7. ĕl′ ò eū′ tion	13. lĕe′ tùre
2. mĭs′ sĭle	8. ŏb′ lò quў	14. lĕġ′ ĭ ble
3. ăd mĭt′	9. vĕn trĭl′ ò quĭst	15. lē′ ġiòn
4. dĭs mĭss′	10. măn′ û al	16. eŏl′ lĕġe
5. prŏm′ ĭse	11. măn′ û serĭpt	17. eū′ lò ġĭze
6. ĕm′ ĭs sâ rў	12. ē măn′ çĭ pāte	18. dĭl′ ĭ ġent

DEFINITION. 1 means an errand; the business on which one is sent. 2, a weapon thrown. 3, to allow to enter; to acknowledge as true. 4, to send away. 5, a declaration by which one binds himself to do or not to do some particular act. 6, an agent sent out to advance his employers' interests. 7, the act of speaking or reading in public. 8, reproach, censure. 9, one who speaks so that his voice seems not to come from him but from some other source. 10, done by hand; a book of such size that it may be easily carried in the hand. 11, written by hand. 12, to set free. 13, a discourse on any subject. 14, capable of being read. 15, a multitude. 16, a school for the higher studies. 17, to praise. 18, attentive, laborious, industrious.

LESSON CCLXXXIV.

Words hard to spell and their meaning.

sóm' ẽr saᵤlt — A leap in which a person turns heels over head and lights upon his feet.

eẖlŏ' rŏ fôrm — A chemical used in surgical operations to produce loss of feeling.

mär' tial (-shɑl) — Of, or suited for, war; military.

prăe' tĭ eȧ ble — That may be done, practiced or accomplished.

heärth — The floor in a chimney on which a fire is made; home.

brĭs' tle (brĭs' sl) — A short, stiff hair, as that of swine.

dĕl' ĭ eȧ çў̆ — Delightfulness; refinement.

çў̆l' ĭn dẽr — A body of rollerlike form.

ĭn ĭ' tĭ āte (-ĭsh' ĭ āt) — To begin or enter upon.

eẖăṣm — A deep opening, as in the earth or in a rock.

pẽr suade' (-swăd') — To convince; to win over.

ȧ eăd' ê mў̆ — An institution for the study of higher learning.

ŏe elĕ' ṣĭ ăₛ' tĭe — A priest.

pneû măt' ĭe — Consisting of, or resembling, air.

eoŭr ā' ġeoŭs — Brave; bold.

ȧ pŏth' ê eȧ rў̆ — One who prepares and sells drugs.

ĭn'ĕx hạust' ĭ ble — Incapable of being used up.

pẽr ni' cious (-nĭsh' ŭs) — Destructive; deadly; hateful.

răg' ȧ mŭf' fĭn — A disreputable fellow.

ĕx' ê erȧ ble — Detestable; abominable.

ĭn dĕồt' ĕd — Brought into debt.

eăl' loŭs — Hardened; unfeeling.

LESSON CCLXXXV.

The suffix *ward* (pronounced wẽrd) denotes *motion toward;* *ance* or *ence* (pronounced ans or ens) means *the act* or *state of;* *ure* signifies *state of; ous, eous, ious* mean *having, relating to.*

băck' ward	ĕl' ė gançe	vẽrd' ûre	vĭr' tû oŭs
hōme' ward	pĕn' ĭ tençe	răpt' ûre	pĭt' ė oŭs
down' ward	ȧ bŭn' dançe	ĭm pŏst' ûre	ĕn' vĭ oŭs
ȧft' ẽr ward	eleȧr' ançe	eûr' vȧ tûre	eŭm' broŭs
nôrth' ward	ŏe eûr' rençe	fĭ' broŭs	eoûr' tė oŭs

LESSON CCLXXXVI.

The suffixes *kin, ling, el, le, let, et, ow,* and *ule* mean *little.*

pĭp' kĭn	found' lĭng	bul' lĕt	hăłch' ĕt
lămb' kĭn	sēed' lĭng	eye' lĕt	rĭv' û lĕt
măn' ĭ kĭn	dăm' şĕl	elŏş' ĕt	hŏl' lŏw
gŏş' lĭng	săłch' ĕl	lēaf' lĕt	pĭl' lŏw
där' lĭng	nŏz' zle	hăm' lĕt	mĕad' ŏw
yēar' lĭng	rĭng' lĕt	lăłch' ĕt	glŏb' ûle
dŭck' lĭng	strēam' lĕt	eȧsk' ĕt	ăn' ĭ măl' eûle

LESSON CCLXXXVII.

Words often mispronounced or improperly accented.

ȧ pŏs' łle	ĕ' gȯ tĭşm	läugh' (läf'-) tẽr
ăt' rȯ phў	ĕ' quȧ ble	lў çė' ŭm
au' tŏp sў	ĕx' plė tĭve	lû' dĭ eroŭs
eȧis' sŏn	glä' çiẽr (-shẽr)	mû lė tēer'
ehŏl' ẽr le	hŏs' łler	ȯ bēi' sançe
drä' mȧ	ĭn' tė gral	pû' pĭl lȧ rў
dė' (dȧ') brĭs'	ĭn' vĕn tȯ rў	răil' lẽr ў
dė' (dȧ') but'	ĭn tẽr' stĭçe	rĕş' ĭn oŭs
drouģht	jû' vė nĭle	rĕp' ȧ rȧ ble
dĭ plŏ' mȧ	kże' dĭve	sȯ' joûrn ẽr

LESSON CCLXXXVIII. Synonyms.

These words are to be distinguished carefully from one another.

neglect
slight
We *neglect* from forgetfulness or oversight; we *slight* from a feeling of dislike or contempt. *Neglect* is commonly applied to things; as, to *neglect* duty, to *neglect* business, to *neglect* to pay our debts; *slight*, to persons. A friend may *neglect* us in the hurry of business; but when he *slights* us, it is evident he is our friend no longer.

noted
notorious
Noted may be employed in a good or a bad sense; *notorious* is never used except in a bad sense. A man may be *noted* for his genius, talent, or eccentricities; he is *notorious* for his vices. We speak of a *noted* orator; a *notorious* scamp.

object
oppose
To *object* to a thing is to propose or start something against it; to *oppose* it is to set one's self up steadily against it. One *objects* to ordinary matters that require no reflection; one *opposes* matters that call for deliberation and afford serious reasons for and against. A father *objects* to his son playing in the streets; we *oppose* a law that we believe will not prove for the welfare of the people.

opinion
sentiment
An *opinion* is the result of experience, reflection, or reading; *sentiment* is the consequence of habits and circumstances. An *opinion* is the work of the head; *sentiment* is the work of the heart. We define our *sentiments* on questions of feeling or taste; we give our *opinions* on questions of science and argument.

pardon
forgive
Pardon is the serious style; *forgive* is the familiar term. Men *forgive* one another personal offences; a magistrate *pardons* offences against law.

LESSON CCLXXXIX. Punctuation, Continued.

The **Note of Interrogation** (?) must be placed,—

After every direct question; as,

> Where are you going?

The **Colon** (:) should be used,—

Where a sentence might be considered as finished, but is followed by something without which the full force of the remark would be lost; as,

> Study to acquire a habit of thinking : no study is more important.

Before a direct quotation; as,

> A good motto is : "Do unto others as you would that they should do unto you."

After the adverbs *yes* or *no*, when they form part of the answer to a question; as,

> Are you going to the country? Yes : next week.

After the salutation in a letter; as,

> Reverend, dear Sir :

The **Semicolon** (;) should be used,—

To separate the main divisions of a sentence the subdivisions of which are separated by commas; as,

> Prosperity is naturally, though not necessarily, attached to virtue and merit; adversity, to vice and folly.

To separate a sentence consisting of several members, each constituting a distinct proposition, but having a dependence on each other; as,

> Everything grows old ; everything passes away ; everything disappears.

Before *as, viz., to wit, namely, i. e.,* or *that is*, when they introduce an example; as,

> Many words are differently spelled in English ; as, cigar, segar ; inquire, enquire ; center, centre.

LESSON CCXC. Hard words found in a Third Reader.
To be written by the pupils.

naught	wharf	worthy	especially
foliage	dumb	martyr	acquaintance
. biscuit	vision	surplice	musicians
growth	whence	millions	handkerchief
badges	throne	chaplain	almsgiving

LESSON CCXCI. Hard words from a Third Reader.
To be written by the pupils.

thrives	pshaw	weapon	essential
zealous	blithe	various	convenient
quaint	wreck	bouquet	petitioned
stomach	busily	amiable	associated
ghastly	mingle	disguise	opportunity

LESSON CCXCII. Hard words found in a Third Reader.
To be written by the pupils.

gracious	chasms	whim	separated
brilliant	wrought	lodged	cathedral
microscope	·symbol	dangled	rejoicing
steadfast	knowledge	kernels	murderous
beauteous	contempt	courteous	atmosphere

LESSON CCXCIII. Hard words found in a Third Reader.
To be written by the pupils.

monarch	radiance	nourishment	stiffened
bargain	packages	Esquimaux	generosity
guileless	suspicious	remarkable	exhausted
turbulent	occasions	simplicity	assumption
precipices	delicious	cavalcade	delicacies
diamonds	conditions	missionaries	originated

LESSON CCXCIV. Synonyms.

These words are to be distinguished carefully from one another.

compliment flattery	Men deal in *compliments* from a desire to please; they use *flattery* either from excessive admiration or to gratify vanity.
chastise punish	We *chastise* to prevent the repetition of faults, and to reclaim the offender; we *punish* to uphold the law by the infliction of penalty.
competent qualified	A man is *competent* to a task or duty when he has the powers which are needed for its performance; he is *qualified* for it when those powers have been trained into an acquaintance with the work to be done and expertness in the mode of performing it.
cautious circumspect	*Cautious* denotes a prudent care in avoiding danger; a man who is *circumspect* examines all the circumstances of a case so as carefully to consider them; a brute may be *cautious*, but only rational beings are *circumspect.*
communicate impart reveal	*Communicate* denotes the allowance of others to partake or enjoy *in common* with ourselves; *impart* is giving to others a *part* of what we had held as our own; *reveal* is to disclose something hidden or concealed. For example, we *communicate* intelligence; *impart* instruction; *reveal* a secret.
conceal disguise secrete	To *conceal* is simply not to make known what we wish to keep secret; to *disguise* is to conceal by some false appearance; to *secrete* is to hide in some place of secrecy. Crimes are *concealed*; we often *disguise* our sentiments; stolen goods are *secreted.*

LESSON CCXCV. Latin Roots.

moveo, motum = *to move;* **munus** = *a gift;* **litera** = *a letter;*
locus = *a place.*

1. rê mọve'
2. rê mōte'
3. ê mō' tion
4. mọv' á ble
5. prô mō' tion
6. eŏm mūn' ion

7. ĭm mū' nĭ tỹ
8. mû nĭf' ĭ çençe
9. rê mū' nēr ăte
10. eŏm mū' nĭ tỹ
11. eŏm mū' nĭ eäte
12. ĭl lĭt' ēr ăte

13. lĕt' tēr
14. lĭt' ēr al
15. lĭt' ēr á tûre
16. lō' eal
17. lō' eäte
18. lō' eô mō' tĭve

DEFINITION. 1 means to change place in any manner. 2, far away. 3, feeling, agitation. 4, capable of being moved. 5, advanced in rank or honor. 6, the Blessed Sacrament; unity. 7, freedom from any duty or obligation. 8, excessive generosity. 9, to reward, to repay. 10, common possession or enjoyment; a body of people having common rights. 11, to make known. 12, uneducated. 13, a mark or character used to represent a sound; a written or printed communication. 14, real. 15, learning, science. 16, belonging to one particular place. 17, to place, to settle. 18, moving from place to place.

LESSON CCXCVI. Latin Roots.

ars, artis = *art;* **centum** = *a hundred;* **decem** = *ten;*
dens, dentis = *tooth.*

1. ärt' ĭst
2. ĭn ērt'
3. ĭn ēr' ti a (shĭ á)
4. är' tĭ şăn
5. ärt' lĕss
6. är' tĭ fĭçe

7. çĕn' tû rỹ
8. çĕn tū' rĭ òn
9. çĕn tĕn' nĭ al
10. çĕn' tĭ pĕd
11. pēr çĕnt' áġe
12. dĕç' ĭ mal

13. dĕç' ĭ mǎte
14. dĕç' ĭ mǎl lỹ
15. dĕnt
16. ĭn dĕnt'
17. trĭ' dent
18. dĕn' tal

DEFINITION. 1 means one who professes and practices an art. 2, dull, lifeless. 3, indisposition to motion. 4, a mechanic. 5, simple, unaffected. 6, a skillful contrivance; a trick. 7, a hundred years. 8, a captain of a hundred men. 9, happening once in a hundred years. 10, an insect with a great number of feet. 11, the interest, commission, etc., on a hundred. 12, numbered by tens. 13, to take the tenth part. 14, by tens. 15, a slight notch or hollow, as if made by pressure of a tooth. 16, to stamp or to press in. 17, a kind of spear with three prongs. 18, relating to the teeth.

LESSON CCXCVII. Homonyms.

eŏm′plê ment, that which completes.

eŏm′ plĭ ment, praise; flattery;

sĕll, to give in exchange for money.

çĕll, a small, close room, as in a prison.

çĕnt, a piece of money.

sĕnt, caused to go.

scĕnt, to smell.

dēar, highly valued; greatly loved.

dēer, an animal.

dew(dū), condensed moisture from the air.

dūe, owed.

dōe, a female deer.

dōugh, paste of bread.

fâir, clear; open; spotless.

fâre, the price of passage or going.

foul, dirty.

fowl (foul), a bird.

greāt, big, grand.

grāte, a frame of iron bars for holding a fire.

hēel, the hinder part of the foot.

hēal, to cure of a disease or wound.

LESSON CCXCVIII. Dictation Exercise.

A compliment is often a lie in fine clothes. Our regiment has its complement of men. I can scent the perfume of the flower even from this distance. The prison cell is cold and damp. The fare on the car is more than a cent. The dew is falling heavily. I sent my son to get some money that is due to me. The price I asked for the deer and the doe was not too dear. Wild fowl are sweet eating. The child's skin is fair. The water is foul. A sore heel is hard to heal. There is a great hot fire in the grate. I will sell my house if I can find a buyer.

LESSON CCXCIX. *Gh* and *ph* with the sound of *f*.

toŭgh	roŭgh	trŏugh	dràught
eough (kạf)	läugh	sloŭgh	çǐ' phēr
soŭgh	eloŭgh	ê noŭgh'	phўş' ĭe
glўph	sўlph	sŭl' phŭr	nĕph' ew (-û)

LESSON CCC.

Words frequently mispronounced or improperly accented.

fĕt' ĭd	jeān	phä' ê tŏn	tĕn' ĕt
fĭ' nĭte	jă guär'	prŏg' rĕss	tĭ räde'
fĭ' (fê)nĕsse'	lĭs' ten	prò lĭx'	tō' ward (- ērd)
gäunt	mĕt' rĭe	rọu ẹ'	vĭs' eount'
glä' mọur	nä' ĭve	rĕt' ĭ nà	vō' eà ble
ghọul	pê' ô nў	säun' tēr	wĕap' òn
hụr räh'	pĕt' al	stànch	yạcht
hăr' ass	prē' lŭde	sä' lĭ ent	ăs' sĕts
hòv' ēr	pū' ēr ĭle	sä' chem	eū' pò là
ĭ tăl' ĭe	prō' tê an	sŏf' ten	eô' te riê'

LESSON CCCI.

Words frequently mispronounced or improperly accented.

mēr' eăn tĭle	· rĕv' ēr ĭe	ăl tēr' nàte
măr' ĭ tĭme	rĕç' ĭ prŏç' ĭ tў	ăb stē' mĭ oŭs
mạu sò lē' ŭm	rĕp' ēr tô rў	ăp pĕl' là tĭve
mĕl lĭf' lù oŭs	sáe' rĭ lē' gioŭs	ăe çĕl' ēr à tĭve
mnê mŏn' ĭe	sĭ' nê eūre	bär bär' ĭe
ôr'ehĕs tral	sŭb sĭd' ençe	çhăs' tĭşe ment
prŏe' ù rä tôr	sà lū' tà tô rў	eôr' ŏl là rў
pū' ĭs sançe	spŏn tà nē' ĭ tў	dê făl' eàte
pĕr' ĕmp tô rў	strўeh' nĭne	dĕs' pĭ eà ble
prĕş' bў tēr ў	sehĕd' ûle	ĕn frän' çhĭşe
prê çĕp' tô rў	stò mäeh' ĭe	ĕp ĭ zō' ô tў

LESSON CCCII. Punctuation, Continued.

The **Dash** (—) is used,—

To mark an abrupt turn in a sentence or before a word or phrase repeated for the purpose of emphasis; as,

> The faithful man acts not from impulse, but from conviction—conviction of duty.

Instead of a parenthesis; as,

> Religion—who can doubt it?—is the noblest of themes.

The **Parenthesis** ( ) is used,—

To enclose an expression inserted in the body of a sentence containing some information which may be omitted without affecting the sense; as,

> Know then this truth (enough for man to know),
> Virtue alone is happiness below.

Brackets [ ] are used,—

To enclose some correction or explanation; as,

> When I walked away he [my brother] followed me.

Quotation Marks (" ") are used,—

To show that the exact words of a speaker are given; as,

> "God is love," says St. Paul.

The **Apostrophe** (') is used,—

To show the omission of a letter or of letters; as,

> If I'd a throne, I'd freely share it with thee.

To denote the possessive case; as,

> The priest's breviary.

The **Hyphen** (-) is used,—

To connect the parts of compound words, or to connect parts of a word divided at the end of a line; as,

> The all-wise God.

LESSON CCCIII.
Words hard to spell and their meaning.

ĭn ạu' gŭ rāte — To introduce into an office with suitable ceremonies.

ū' tĭl ĭze — To make useful.

ăm' bŭ lançe — A moving hospital attached to an army; a wagon for removing the sick or wounded.

rĕs' tau (-tô-) rànt — An eating house.

seĥô lăs' tĭe — Scholarlike; a novice, in some religious Order, who has taken his first vows.

mĭn' strĕl sў — The singing and playing of minstrels or musicians.

stĭg' mȧ tȧ — Marks in imitation of the wounds of Our Saviour supernaturally impressed upon the bodies of certain persons.

ĭn ê' brĭ āte — To make drunk.

trȧ ġê' dĭ ạn — A writer of tragedy; an actor or player in tragedy.

hê rĕd' ĭ tȧ rў — Come down from an ancestor to an heir; from a parent to a child.

ĕn dĕav' or (-ẽr) — To try.

ăb' ô lĭ' tion (-lĭsh' ŭn) — The act of putting an end to; destruction.

ĭd' ĭ ô çў — Absence of sense and intelligence.

seĥĕd' ûle — A written or printed sheet of paper; a list prepared for legal or business purposes.

dĭph'(-dĭf'-) thŏng — A union of two vowels in one syllable.

mĕn ăg'(ăzh') ẽr ĭe — A place where animals are kept.

LESSON CCCIV. Homonyms.

a*ught*, anything.

ou*ght*, should.

ȧnt, an insect.

äʉnt, the sister of one's father or mother.

a̤l' tar (-tĕr), a place on which a sacrifice is offered.

a̤l' tĕr, to change.

bow, a bending of the body, out of respect.

bou*gh*, a branch of a tree.

brĕd, brought up.

brĕ*ad*, an article of food.

blūe, the color of the sky.

blew, produced a current of air.

choir (kwīr), a band of church singers.

quire (kwīr), twenty-four sheets of paper.

cōre, the heart or inner part of a thing.

cōr*ps*, a body of men.

coun' sĕl, advice.

coun' çĭl, an assembly.

cōarse, thick; rough.

cōurse, road; passage.

LESSON CCCV. Dictation Exercise.

A church without an altar is an empty house. The ant is held up to us as a model of industry. Our church has a very good choir. The wind blew so hard that a bough was broken off the big tree. The sky is blue, but the clouds are of many colors. Fred is a well-bred boy; he made a pretty bow when I met him in the street. The city council ought to give free bread to the poor. For aught I know, my aunt took counsel of no one, but made up her mind to alter her house to suit herself. Our regiment is a fine corps. The apple is rotten at the core. I want a quire of coarse, brown paper. The course of the ship took it into stormy waters.

LESSON CCCVI. Synonyms.

These words are to be distinguished carefully from one another.

attend
accompany
We *accompany* those with whom we go as companions; we *attend* those whom we wait upon; as, I shall *accompany* my mother to the city, so as to *attend* to her.

abstinence
temperance
Total *abstinence* is the right thing for those who cannot practice *temperance*.

ancient
antiquated
Ancient is opposed to *modern;* as, *ancient* heroes; *antiquated* describes that which has gone out of use; as, the furniture is *antiquated*.

advantage
benefit
We speak of a thing as a *benefit* when we gain or profit by it; as an *advantage* when it affords us the means of getting forward; as, the support of friends is an *advantage;* good health is an inestimable *benefit*.

adjacent
adjoining
Things are *adjacent* when they lie near to each other without actually touching; as, *adjacent* villages; what is *adjoining* must touch at some point; as, *adjoining* farms.

accomplish
achieve
effect
execute
We *accomplish* an object, as, my brother was able to *accomplish* his proposed work; we *achieve* an enterprise or undertaking of some importance; *effect* a purpose; *execute* a design, project, or the orders of others.

abolish
annul
repeal
revoke
Abolish applies to institutions, usages, customs, etc.; as to *abolish* slavery. *Annul* denotes simply to make void, to reduce to nothing; as, to *annul* a contract. *Repeal* describes the act by which a law is set aside. *Revoke* denotes the act of recalling some previous grant which conferred power.

LESSON CCCVII. *Ph* with the sound of *f*.

phĭz	phăn' tòm	blăs phĕme'	phĕ' nĭx
sphēre	prŏph' ĕt	phär' mȧ çў	tĕl' ê grȧph
phrāṣe	trī' ŭmph	ĕl' ê phant	phĭ lŏs' ô phў
nўmph	grăph' ĭe	ạu' tô grȧph	phŏs' phŏr oŭs
phlĕgm	eăm' phīne	dĭph' thŏng	eăm' phor (-fēr)
sphĭṇx	môr' phīne	tĕl' ê phōne	phў ṣīque' (-zēk)
sĕr' aph	păm' phlĕt	phô nĕt' ĭe	eăl lĭg' rȧ phў

LESSON CCCVIII. Silent *l*, *n*, and final *ue*.

ălmṣ	stạlk	lĭmn	vāgue
bạlk	chạlk	dămn	vōgue
bälm	psälm	eŏl' ŭmn	brōgue
eạlk	hўmn	sŏl' ĕmn	lẽague
pälm	fạl' eon	eŏn dĕmn'	plāgue
eọuld	sälm' ȯn	quälm (kwäm)	tôngue
fōlks	kĭln	rōgue	fȧ tïgue

LESSON CCCIX.

Words frequently mispronounced or improperly accented.

ȧ mĕn' ĭ tў	chăr' ĭ ŏt ēer'	ĭn tẽr' pô lāte
ăv' oĭr dû poiṣ'	eŏm' plâi ṣănçe	ĭn ŭn' dāte
ăd' vẽrse lў	drowned	ĭn eŏm' pȧ rȧ ble
ăg' grăn dīze	dê lĭb' ēr ȧ tïve	ĭr rĕf' rȧ gȧ ble
băp' tĭs tẽr ў	ĕm' pў rē' an	ĭr rĕp' ȧ rȧ ble
eạọuí' chọue	ĕx traôr' dĭ nȧ rў	ĭr rĕv' ô eȧ ble
eŏn sĭs' tô rў	Fĕb' rụ ȧ rў	ĭn dĭs' pụ tȧ ble
eŏn sŏl' ȧ tô rў	găr' rụ loŭs	ĭn dĭs' sô lû ble
çhĭv' al rĭe	grĭĕv' oŭs	ĭn ĕx' ô rȧ ble
eŏm' băt ĭve	hў'mê nē' al	ĭn ĕx' plĭ eȧ ble
eŏm' mû nĭst	ĭl lûs' trāte	ĭg nĭt' ĭ ble

LESSON CCCX. Words hard to spell and their meaning.

bė trŏthed′(-trŏtht′)	Engaged in marriage.
á grēe′ á ble	Pleasing; grateful.
bĭl′ liards (-yērdz)	A game played with ivory balls.
ăd mĭs′ sĭ ble	Worthy of being admitted.
eoun′ sĕl or (-ēr)	One who gives advice; one who pleads in a court of law.
mĭn′ ĭ á tûre	A very small picture, especially a portrait; something small.
dĭ vĭş′ ĭ ble	Capable of being divided.
bụl′ lė tĭn	An official account of public news; any public announcement of recently received news.
ġȳm nä′ şĭ ŭm	A place for muscular exercise; a school for instruction in the higher branches of learning.
băn′ quet (-kwĕt)	A feast.
sē′ erê çў	The state of being hidden.
ăe quaint′(-kwänt′-)ançe	Familiarity; intimacy.
prŏe′ lá mä′ tion	That which is publicy announced.
vĭl′ laĭn	A vile, wicked person; a rascal.
ăn′ ĕe dŏte	A particular fact of an interesting nature.
eá thē′ dral	The principal church in a diocese.
lä′ ĭ tў	The people, as distinguished from the clergy.
mė′tė or (-ēr)	Any appearance in the atmosphere, as clouds, rain, hail.
lạud′ á ble	Worthy of being praised.
nŏe tûr′ nal	Belonging to, done, or occurring in the night.

LESSON CCCXI. Synonyms.

These words are to be distinguished carefully from one another.

persevere
persist
continue
To *persevere* is to be steady throughout to the end; to *persist* is to continue from a determination not to give up; to *continue* is simply to do as one has done heretofore. We *continue* the conversation that was interrupted; if the girl *perseveres* in her studies she will be the first in her class; if the man *persists* in doing wrong he will be arrested.

pagan
heathen
heretic
Pagan is applied to any rude and uncivilized people who worship false gods; *heathen* to all who practice idolatry; and *heretic* to baptized, professing Christians who believe or practice doctrines not approved by the Catholic Church. The South Sea Islanders are *pagans;* the Persians are *heathens;* Protestants are *heretics.*

permanent
durable
Permanent applies to things not likely to fail or change; *durable* is applied to material substances so formed as to be fitted to last long. For example, my brother has a situation which is likely to prove *permanent;* the house is built of *durable* material.

pertinacity
obstinacy
Pertinacity denotes great firmness in holding on to a thing; *obstinacy* is a resolute attachment to one's own way of thinking or acting. For example, the king showed his *obstinacy* by refusing to listen to advice, and the result was war; the inventor by his *pertinacity* in keeping to work finally perfected the machine.

perceive
discern
We *perceive* that which is obvious; we *discern* that which is remote or requires much attention to get an idea of it. We *perceive* light, darkness, colors, or the truth or falsehood of any thing; we *discern* characters, motives, etc.

LESSON CCCXII. *C* with the sound of *k*.

ꝫeōre	ăe′ tòr	mò ꞩā′ ie	eăt′ à răet
elēan	eòl′ òr	dēa′ eon	ŏe′ stà sӯ
seāre	ăt′ tїe	dŏe′ trїne	frăe′ tion
serēam	bā′ eon	făe′ tò rӯ	eŏm′ mērçe
seāle	gŏth′ ie	eăl′ ı eồ	vồ eā′ tion

LESSON CCCXIII. *C* with the sound of *s*.

lāçe	pär′ çĕl	eăn′ çĕl	çē′ rê al
grāçe	ăç′ ıd	eoun′ çїl	păç′ ı fӯ
spїçe	grō′ çēr	sїn çēre′	rê çıt′ al
dànçe	pĕn′ çїl	jŭs′ tїçe	prїn′ çї pal
dē′ çĕnt	dê çıde′	chăl′ ïçe	çē′ dar (-dēr)

LESSON CCCXIV.

The suffixes *able* and *ible* mean *that which may or can be*. Words ending in *e* usually drop the *e* before a termination beginning with an *a* or an *o*, except after *c* and *g*.

ēat′ à ble	ê răs′ à ble	lĕg′ ı ble	plạu′ ꞩї ble
sāl′ à ble	tēach′ à ble	fū′ ꞩı ble	ïn dĕl′ ı blє
pāy′ à ble	läugh′ à ble	rїꞩ′ ı ble	ïn vїꞩ′ ı ble
eūr′ à ble	trāçe′ à ble	sĕn′ sı ble	dї vїꞩ′ ı ble
tăm′ à ble	chärġe′ à ble	ĕd′ ı blє	dї ġĕst′ ı ble
lòv′ à ble	dê fїn′ à ble	fōr′ çı ble	dïf fū′ ꞩı ble
tăx′ à ble	ăm′ ı eà ble	hŏr′ rї ble	rê vērs′ ı ble
mọv′ à ble	rê çĕïv′ à ble	tĕr′ rї ble	pēr çĕp′ tї ble
rēad′ à ble	mїꞩ′ ēr à ble	erĕd′ ı ble	eŏn vērt′ ı ble
blām′ à ble	ăd vїꞩ′ à ble	flĕx′ ı ble	ăd mїs′ sї ble
fōrd′ à ble	dê tĕst′ à ble	ạu′ dї ble	ïm prĕss′ ı ble
pàss′ à ble	ŏb tāіn′ à ble	făl′ lї ble	ïm pŏs′ sї ble
beăr′ à ble	ŏb ꞩērv′ à ble	tăn′ ġї ble	ĕx haụst′ ı blє

LESSON CCCXV. Homonyms.

one (wŭn), a single unit; single.

wŏn (wŭn), did win.

ŏh, an exclamation of pain or sorrow.

ŏwe, to be bound to pay.

ŏde, a short, dignified poem or song.

ŏwed, did owe.

pŏur, to cause a liquid to flow out of or into a vessel.

pŏre, a small opening.

prieș, peeps into that which is closed.

prīze, that which is won.

pĕaçe, a state of quiet.

piĕçe, a part of any thing.

prāy, to ask for a favor; to entreat; to supplicate.

prey, plunder; booty.

prāyș, supplicates.

prāișe, honor; applause.

preyș, takes by force.

plŭm, a fruit.

plŭmb, perpendicular.

plăçe, location; site; spot.

plăiçe, a fish.

plĕașe, to be willing, as a favor.

plĕaș, excuses.

LESSON CCCXVI. Dictation Exercise.

My sister's ode won great praise and took the prize. Oh, how glad I would be if I did not owe one cent. I have paid off the mortgage I owed on my place. Please pour a cup of tea for me. The perspiration ran from every pore of my body. To work is to pray. Peace has more victories than war. Charles was carrying a piece of plum pie when he fell. The tiger is a beast of prey. The gate sags because it is not plumb. The plaice is a flat fish. The child prays devoutly. Man preys on his fellowman. Under the pleas of overseeing and of duty, that man pries into every one's business.

LESSON CCCXVII. Synonyms.

These words are to be distinguished carefully from one another.

faultless
blameless
We speak of a thing as *faultless* when it is free from defects as well as from evil; as *blameless* when it is free from evil or wickedness alone. Thus we say: He led a *blameless* life; the organist's playing was *faultless*.

freedom
liberty
Freedom is personal and private; *liberty*, public. We say, *freedom* of will or conversation; *liberty* of conscience, of the press. *Freedom*, moreover, serves to qualify the action; *liberty* is applied only to the agent; hence we say, to speak with *freedom*, but to have the *liberty* of speaking.

fiction
fabrication
Fiction is opposed to what is real, *fabrication* to what is true. *Fiction* serves to amuse and instruct; *fabrication* to mislead and deceive. Sir Walter Scott was a master of *fiction;* the poems of Ossian are *fabrications* by Macpherson.

fear
dread
apprehension
Fear creates anxiety; *dread*, wretchedness; *apprehension*, uneasiness. We *fear* a misfortune; we *dread* a calamity; we *apprehend* an unpleasant occurrence.

foe
enemy
adversary
opponent
antagonist
A *foe* bears hatred; an *enemy* is unfriendly; an *adversary* takes part against another in a contest; an *opponent* is pitted against another; an *antagonist* struggles against another. For example, our passions, when indulged, are our *enemies;* envy is a *foe* to happiness; my sister was my *adversary* in the game of chess; my brother's *opponent* in the debate was an able man; the juniors and the freshmen were *antagonists* in the ball game.

LESSON CCCXVIII.   Words hard to spell and their meaning.

*e*ĥôrd	A term used in music.
dĭse	A flat round plate.
*g*nōm*e*	A dwarf; an imaginary being, such as goblin.
plä*gue*	To tease.
se*ĥ*ēm*e*	A plan; a system.
mĭs′ chĭê voŭs	Harmful; hurtful.
heī*gh*t	The distance to which anything rises above that on which it stands.
slou*gh*	A place of deep mud.
drou*gh*t	Dryness; want of rain or of water.
ôr′ *e*ĥĕs trâ	The musicians performing in a theatre, hall, or other place of public amusement.
är′ *e*ĥĭ tĕet	One skilled in the art of building.
fâ tīg*ue*′	Weariness caused by exertion of body or mind.
*e*oun′tẽr feĭt′	A copy intended to be passed off for an original.
a*n*′ *e*ĥor (-kĕr-)â*g*e	A place suitable for anchoring.
phär′ (-fär′·) mâ çy	A drug store.
sŏl′ ĕm*n*	Grave; serious.
pôr′ pòis*e*	A species of fish.
â pŏs′ tâ sȳ	A total desertion of one's faith or principles.
plŭm*b*′ ēr	One who works in lead.
*e*oûr′tê oŭs	Well bred; polite.
lĕg′ â çȳ	A gift of property by will.
ê lĕe trĭç′ ĭ tȳ	A power in nature.
dê lĭr′ ĭ oŭs .	Insane; wandering in mind.

LESSON CCCXIX.

The suffix *fy* means *to make; ion, the act of* or *the state of being;* and *ive, the quality* or *nature of.*

săt′ ĭs fȳ	dĭ vẽr′ sion	ĕx plō′ şion	à bū′ sĭve
făl′ sĭ fȳ	ĕx çĕp′ tion	eŏn dĭ′ tion	ĭl lū′ sĭve
ăm′ plĭ fȳ	ăs pẽr′ sion	dĭf fū′ şion	ê lĕet′ ĭve
sĭm′ plĭ fȳ	ăt tĕn′ tion	dĭs pẽr′ şion	ĕx tĕn′ sĭve
elăs′ sĭ fȳ	dè çĭ′ şion	ăt trăe′ tion	ŏf fĕn′ sĭve
beaū′ tĭ fȳ	ăd hĕ′ şion	eŏn strŭe′ tion	pẽr çĕp′ tĭve
ĭn tĕn′ sĭ fȳ	ĕx elū′ şion	sŭb mĭs′ sĭve	ĭn vĕnt′ ĭve
ê lĕe′ tion	dè lū′ şion	eŏn elū′ sĭve	prê vĕnt′ ĭve

LESSON CCCXX.
The English prefix *a* means *on, in, at, of, to, for.*

à sĭde′	à lŏft′	à slănt′	à strĭde′
à fĭre′	à hĕad′	à drĭft′	à flōat′
à strāy′	à slĕep′	à bōard′	à ground′

LESSON CCCXXI.
The English prefix *en* means *to make;* in some words, for the sake of ease in pronunciation, it is changed to *em*. *En* also means *in* or *into,* and the Latin prefix *in* means the same. *In* sometimes has a negative meaning; it is often changed to *il, ir, im,* and *ig* to make the sound more pleasing to the ear.

ĕn lärġe′	ĕm bŏd′ ў	ĭn eŭl′ eáte	ĭm brųe′
ĕn trēat′	ĕm pow′ ẽr	ĭn aų′ gù rāte	ĭm pĭnġe′
ĕn tĭ′ tle	ĕm bōld′ en	ĭl lū′ mĭne	ĭm mẽrse′
ĕn nŏ′ ble	ĕm bĭt′ tẽr	ĭl lŭs′ trĭ oŭs	ĭm pẽr′ ĭl
ĕn tăṉ′ gle	ĭn çĭte′	ĭr′ rĭ gāte	ĭm prĭş′ on
ĕn fĕჳ′ ble	ĭn′ bôrn	ĭr rŭp′ tion	ĭm′ mĭ grāte
ĕn dăn′ ġẽr	ĭn elĭne′	ĭr rä′ dĭ àte	ĭg nŏ′ ble
ĕn eoŭr′ âġe	ĭn elūde′	ĭm pärt′	ĭg′ nô rant
ĕn răp′ tûre	ĭn çĕn′ tĭve	ĭm bĭbe′	ĭg′ nô mĭn′ ў

LESSON CCCXXII. Latin Roots.

bene = *good;* **beatus** = *blessed;* **claudo, clausum** = *to close, shut;*
cor = *the heart.*

1. bĕn' ê fĭt	7. bê ăt' ĭ fȳ	13. rê elūse'
2. bĕn' ĭ ṣon	8. bê á tĭf' ĭe	14. ĭn elūde'
3. bê nĕv' ô lent	9. bê ăt' ĭ tūde	15. ĭn elōṣe'
4. bê nĕf'ĭ çent	10. elōṣ' ĕt	16. eōre
5. bĕn ê fáe' tor	11. elois' tēr	17. eŏn̤' eôrd
6. bĕn ê fĭ' cial	12. eŏn elūde'	18. eôr' dial(-jal)

DEFINITION. 1 means a favor conferred; gain. 2, blessing. 3, kind, humane. 4, doing good. 5, one who does good. 6, helpful. 7, to make happy; to declare to be among the blessed though not a Saint. 8, affording heavenly bliss. 9, heavenly joy. 10, a small room for retirement; a closed recess in which household utensils are kept. 11, a convent, a monastery. 12, to finish. 13, one who lives retired from the world. 14, to shut in, to contain. 15, to surround, to shut in. 16, the heart or inner part of anything, particularly of fruit. 17, agreement; peace. 18, sincere, hearty.

LESSON CCCXXIII. Latin Roots.

corpus, corporis = *the body;* **credo, creditum** = *to believe;*
curro, cursum = *to run.*

1. eōrps	7. erēed	13. rê eûr'
2. eôrpse	8. erĕd' ĭt or (-ēr)	14. sŭe'eor(-kēr)
3. eôr' pô ral	9. erĕd' ĭ ble	15. eŭr' rent
4. eôr' pû lent	10. erê dĕn' tial	16. eûr' sô rȳ
5. eŏr pô' rê al	11. dĭs erĕd' ĭt	17. prê eûr' sor
6. ĭn eôr' pô râte	12. ĭn erĕd' û lơŭs	18. ĕx eûr' sion
	19. dĭs eōurse'	20. eŏn eûr'

DEFINITION. 1 means a body of men. 2, a dead body. 3, relating to the body. 4, fat, stout. 5, having a body, not spiritual. 6, to form into a body; to unite. 7, a profession of that which is believed. 8, one to whom a debt is owed. 9, worthy of belief. 10, that upon which belief is claimed. 11, to disbelieve. 12, hard of belief. 13, to return again or repeatedly. 14, help, aid. 15, a running stream. 16, hastily. 17, a forerunner. 18, a going from a place, as in traveling. 19, conversation, talk, speech. 20, to agree, in action or opinion.

LESSON CCCXXIV. Words hard to spell and their meaning.

Ⓒhrĭsʈ′ mɑs   The feast in honor of the birth of our Saviour.

ĕr rō′ nê oŭs   Incorrect; false.

fâ çē′ tious (-shŭs) Witty; humorous.

sãl′ ȧ ble   Fit to be sold.

gŏn′ dô lĭēr′   One who rows a gondola, a peculiar kind of boat.

vĕt′ ẽr ɑn   One old in experience, particularly an old soldier.

hę̄′ noŭs   Hatefully bad.

mū′ çĭ lâge   A gummy substance.

pōul′ tĭçe   A thick pap applied as a plaster to remove inflammation.

vĕnġe′ ɑnçe   Punishment inflicted in return for an injury.

ăd′ âġe   An old saying; a proverb.

bĭ′ ɑsed (-ɑst)   Inclined to one side; prejudiced.

seạl′ lòp   A species of shell-fish.

ĭ tăl′ ĭ çĭze   To print in *Italic* type, that is, type sloping to the right; to underline a letter or word, in writing, with a single line.

eăt′ ȧ lŏgue   A list of names, books, works, etc., arranged in a certain order.

ġy̆p′ sy̆   A name applied to a certain wandering race of people.

sĭ′phŏn (-fŏn)   A pipe or tube used for transferring a liquid from one vessel to another.

ŭn′ ȧ brĭdġed   Complete.

dū′ bĭ oŭs   Doubtful.

mȧ neụ′ vẽr   Skillful management.

LESSON CCCXXV. Synonyms.

These words are to be distinguished carefully from one another.

balance   *Balance* ought not be used for *remainder*. *Bal-*
remainder   *ance* is the excess of one thing over another.
We may speak of the *balance* of an account,
because it is that which makes the two sides
even, or a *balance* at the bank; but we must
say, the *remainder* of the evening, the *remainder*
of the week.

brief   A sentence is *brief* when it is expressed in few
concise   words; it is *concise* when only the necessary
terse   words are used; it is *terse* when it is expressed
with smoothness, grace, or elegance. For ex-
ample, we say, The Senator's speech was *brief*,
occupying only a few minutes; his opponent's
was *concise*, but to the purpose, while that of
the third man was *terse*, and charmed every
one.

benevolence *Benevolence* is the desire of doing good; *benefi-*
beneficence *cence* is the actual goodness; as, the man was
naturally *benevolent*, but owing to the circumstances of his life he could not show any one
very great *beneficence*.

courage   *Courage* meets danger without fear. *Bravery* is
bravery   displayed in daring deeds. *Fortitude* meets
fortitude   danger and enduring pain with a steadfast
and unbroken spirit.

choose   To *choose* is an act of the will; to *prefer* is to
prefer   choose one thing as more desirable than
another, and is an act of judgment; as, to
choose a profession; to *prefer* a private life to
a public one.

character *Character* is the real inner worth of a man;
reputation *reputation* is the world's opinion of him; as,
his *reputation* is not good, but could we see
his real *character*, we should not find him
so bad.

LESSON CCCXXVI.

The English prefix *be* means *to make*.

bė dew'(-dū')	bė fạll'	bė wĭtch'	bė rēave'
bė stĭr'	bė eälm'	bė nŭmb'	bė frĭĕnd'
bė stŏw'	bė eloud'	bė smēar'	bė grŭdġe'
bė dĭm'	bė wäĭl'	bė spēak'	bė fŏgged'

LESSON CCCXXVII.

The English prefixes *mis*, *out*, and *over* mean respectively *wrong* or *wrongly*, *doing in a better manner than*, and *excess* or *superiority*.

mĭs lāy'	mĭs lēad'	mĭs chànçe'	ŏ' vēr ạwe'
mĭs stĕp'	mĭs dĕed'	out bĭd'	.ŏ' vēr eòme'
mĭs rụle'	mĭs spĕnd'	out dâre'	ŏ' vēr chärġe'
mĭs dāte'	mĭs prĭnt'	out brăg'	ŏ' vēr lŏad'
mĭs tāke'	mĭs gụide'	out grŏw'	ŏ' vēr ĭs' sůe
mĭs eạll'	mĭs quōte'	out brăve'	ŏ' vēr zĕal' oůs

LESSON CCCXXVIII.

The English prefix *fore* and the Latin *pre* and *ante* mean *before*. The Greek *anti* means *opposite, against*.

fōre eàst'	prė dĭet'	prė ṣērve'	ăn' tė çĕd' ent
fōre bŏde'	prė ṣĭde'	prė jŭdġe'	ăn' tė päs'eħal
fōre stạll'	prė' tĕxt	prē' mà tūre'	ăn' tĭ dŏte
prė fēr'	prė pâre'	ăn' tė rōŏm	ăn' tĭ pŏde
prė fĭx'	prē' sāġe	ăn' tė dāte	ăn tĭp' à thў

LESSON CCCXXIX. Words accented on the first syllable

brŏ' mĭne	är' tĭ ṣăn	ạl' dēr man	ăb· jĕet nĕss
ăsťħ' mà	ăb' à eŭs	ăn' çĕs tòr	gōoṣe' bĕr rў
grăn' deîr	är' sė nĭe	är' ġĕn tĭne	ăv' à länche
är' à bĭe	ạl' ġė brá	bûr' gŭn dў	blăs' phė moŭs

LESSON CCCXXX. Latin Roots.

debeo, debitum = *to owe;* **decet** = *it is becoming;* **culpa** = *a fault;*
clamo = *to cry out;* **civis** = *a citizen.*

1. dĕb' ĭt
2. dĕŏt' or (-ẽr)
3. dĕ bĕn' tŭre
4. ĭn dĕŏt' ĕd
5. dĕ' çent
6. dĕe' ŏ rāte

7. dĕ eō' roŭs
8. eŭl' prĭt
9. eŭl' på ble
10. ĭn eŭl' pāte
11. elāĭm
12. elăm' or (-ẽr)

13. ĕx elāĭm'
14. prŏ elāĭm'
15. dĕe' lå mā' tion
16. çĭt' y̆
17. çĭv' ĭe
18. çĭv' ĭl

19. çĭ vĭl' ian (-yan)   20. çĭv' ĭ lĭ zā' tion

LESSON CCCXXXI. Latin Roots.

doceo, doctum = *to teach;* **domus** = *a house;* **divinus** = *heavenly;*
durus = *hard.*

1. dŏe' tor (-tẽr)
2. dŏe' trĭne
3. dŏç' ĭle
4. dŏe' ù ment
5. dŏe' trĭ nal
6. dŏe ù mĕn' tå ry̆

7. dōme
8. dŏ mĕs' tĭe
9. dŏm' ĭ çĭle
10. dŏ mĕs' tĭ eāte
11. dĭ vĭne'
12. dĭ vĭn' ĭ ty̆

13. dĭv' ĭ nā' tion
14. dĭ vīne' ly̆
15. ĕn dūre'
16. dūr' ĭng
17. dū' rå ble
18. dù rā' tion

19. ĭn' dù rāte   20. ŏb' dù råt ĕd

LESSON CCCXXXII. Latin Roots.

magnus = *great;* **malus** = *bad;* **modus** = *manner.*

1. mås' tẽr
2. măy̆' or (-ẽr)
3. măg' nĭ fy̆
4. măg' nĭ tūde
5. măg' ĭs trāte
6. må jŏr' ĭ ty̆

7. măg nĭf' ĭ çent
8. măg năn' ĭ moŭs
9. măl' ĭçe
10. măl trēat'
11. må lĕv' ŏ lent
12. må lĭg' nĭ ty̆

13. mōde
14. mŏd' ĕl
15. mŏd' ĕst
16. mŏd' ĭ fy̆
17. mŏd' ẽr āte
18. mŏd' ù lāt

19. eŏm mō' dĭ oŭs   20. ăe eŏm' mŏ dåte

LESSON CCCXXXIII. Synonyms.

These words are to be distinguished carefully from one another.

errand
message
An *errand* is the thing for which one *goes* to a distance; a *message* is the thing for which one is *sent*. A *message* is, properly, any communication which is conveyed; an *errand* sent from one person to another is that which causes one to go. A boy goes the *errand* and delivers the *message*.

enmity
animosity
Enmity lies in the heart; it is deep and malignant. *Animosity* lies in the passions; it is fierce and vindictive. *Enmity* is something permanent; *animosity* is partial and transitory. Thus, we speak of personal *enmity*, fierce *animosity*.

education
instruction
breeding
Education is not alone the communication of knowledge, but also the formation of the mind, the regulation of the heart, and the establishment of correct principles; it belongs to the time of childhood and youth. *Instruction* furnishes the mind with knowledge; it may be given at different ages. *Breeding* relates to the manners or outward conduct; it is best learned in the early part of life.

evidence
testimony
Evidence is whatever makes clear; *testimony* is that which is derived from an individual or a witness. For example, much *testimony* was taken but there was no *evidence* of the commission of a crime.

eternal
endless
What is *eternal* has neither beginning nor end; that which is *endless* has a beginning but no end. Thus we say, God is *eternal;* an *endless* crown of glory in heaven.

expense
cost
The *expense* is that which is laid out for a thing; as, the *expenses* of war. The *cost* is what a thing occasions to be laid out; as, the vase *cost* fifty dollars.

LESSON CCCXXXIV.

The Latin prefixes *a*, *ab*, and *abs* mean *away from*. *Aa,*
ac, af, ag, al, an, ap, ar, as, at mean *to.*

à vērt′	ăd hēre′	ăg griēve′	ăp pạll′
à vāĭl′	ăd dūçe′	ăg′ grà vāte	ăp pēaṣe′
à void′	ăe çēde′	ăl lay′	ăr rīve′
ăb hôr′	ăe eôrd′	ăl lụre′	ăr′ rò gançe
ăb rŭpt′	ăe eount′	ăl lĕġe′	ăs çĕnd′
ăb dŭet′	ăf fĕet′	ăn nĕx′	ăs sīgn′
ăb sŏlve′	ăf fīrm′	ăn nŭl′	ăt trăet′

LESSON CCCXXXV.

The Latin prefix *post* means *after;* the English word is
also used in compounds.

àft′ ẽr nōon	pŏst pōne′	pŏst′ hù moŭs
àft′ ẽr ward (-wẽrd)	pŏst dāte′	pŏst nä′ tal
àft′ ẽr pĭēçe	pŏst′ serĭpt	pŏst nŭp′tial(shal)
àft′ ẽr thought (-thạt)	pŏs tẽr′ ĭ tỹ	pŏst′ mê rīd′ ĭ an

LESSON CCCXXXVI.

The Latin prefix *bi* (from *bis*, twice, which in composition
drops the *s*) means *two, doubly.*

bī′ pĕd	bĭ dĕn′ tal	bĭ lăt′ ẽr al
bĭ sĕet′	bĭ eŭs′ pĭd	bĭ fûr′ eàte
bī′ nàte	bĭ ĕn′ nĭ al	bĭ fō′ lĭ àte
bī′ vălve	bĭ lĭṇ′ gual	bĭ eär′ bŏn àte

LESSON CCCXXXVII.

The prefix *ob* signifies *against*, the letter *b* is often changed
to the first letter of the word to which it is prefixed.

ŏb jĕet′	ŏb trụde′	ŏe eŭlt′	ŏp pōṣe′
ŏb ṣẽrve′	ŏb′ lĭ gāte	ŏe′ eŭ pỹ	ŏp prĕss′
ŏb strŭet′	ŏe eûr′	ŏe eä′ ṣion	ŏp prō′ brĭ ŭm

LESSON CCCXXXVIII. Words often Confounded.

ăf fĕet', to act upon.

ĕf fĕet', result; consequence.

ăd vīçe', counsel.

ăd vīṣe', to counsel; to make known.

ăe çĕpt', to receive; to admit.

ĕx çĕpt', leaving out.

ăr'rant, notorious; vile.

ĕr'rand, message; communion.

ăl'leў, a narrow passage in a city.

ăl lȳ', a confederate.

ăl lū'ṣion, a reference.

ĭl lū'ṣion, a deception.

ăp'pȯ ṣīte, suitable; well adapted.

ŏp'pȯ ṣīte, against; facing.

Brĭt'ȯn, a native of Britain.

Brĭt'ạin, a part of Europe.

băl'lad, a popular song.

băl'lȯt, to vote.

bēa'ẹon, a signal fire.

bĕck'on, to make a sign by nodding or a motion of the hand or finger.

LESSON CCCXXXIX. Dictation Exercise.

I advise you not to take the advice of that man; he is an arrant scamp and the ally of bad people. If you ballot for that candidate the effect will be that it will affect the election. While the boy was going on an errand he was dragged into an alley and robbed. The beacon was reflected in the water on the opposite side of the bay, and the illusion was perfect. Beckon to that waiter. The ballad which the Briton wrote about Great Britain received general praise except from one man who would not accept it as good. His remarks were not apposite, as they contained a personal allusion.

LESSON CCCXL. Synonyms.

These words are to be distinguished carefully from one another.

ridicule To *ridicule* means to expose to, or treat with,
deride   contemptuous laughter; *ridicule* consists
more in words than in actions, and is frequently unaccompanied with any personal
feeling of displeasure; as, to *ridicule* the
fashions of the day. To *deride* also means
to laugh at with contempt, but he who
derides is actuated by a contemptuous spirit;
as, to *deride* one for his religious opinions.

religion *Religion* signifies both a system of faith and
piety   worship, and a sense of duty towards God.
Piety denotes that feeling of veneration and
love which we owe to Him. Our *religion*
teaches us *piety*.

return   We *return* to a person the same as we have
restore received; what we *restore* may or may not
be the same as we have taken, but it ought
to be of equal value. A man *returns* what
he borrowed; he *restores* what he stole.

renowned A person is *renowned* whose name is often
famous   mentioned with honor; he is *famous* who is
distinguished widely spoken of as extraordinary; he is
distinguished who has something which makes
him stand apart from others in the public
view. A man may be *renowned* as a states-
man; *famous* for his eccentricities; and *distinguished* by his abilities or his manners.

source   *Source* is said of that which produces a suc-
origin   cession of objects; *origin* is said of only one
subject. *Source* implies that the supply is
continuous; *origin* that it has ceased. For
example: The *origin* of man is to be traced
to our first parent, Adam; religion is a
never-failing *source* of consolation.

LESSON CCCXLI. Words hard to spell and their meaning

tĭm′ or (-ĕr-) oŭs — Fearful of danger.

thrĕsh′ ōld — The doorsill; entrance; beginning.

ăe′ çĭ dent — An unexpected, undesigned, and sudden event.

ăl′ ꞓō hŏl — Highly rectified spirit.

ēarth′ quake′(-kwāk′) — A shaking or trembling of the earth, often attended with destruction.

ġĕn′ ēr ŏs′ ĭ tў — Nobleness of heart; liberality.

ĭn ꞓŏn tĕst′ á ble — Certain; unquestionable.

nĕg′ lĭ ġençe — Carelessness; heedlessness.

fôrt′ nĭght — Two weeks.

măġ′ ĭs tráte — A public civil officer.

mù nĭç′ ĭ pal — Belonging to a city, state, kingdom, or nation.

Prŏt′ ĕs tant — A Christian who rejects the authority of the Church.

sĭ′ mŭl tā′ nḕ oŭs — Happening at the same time.

ꞓoun′ tḕ nançe — The appearance or expression of the face; encouragement; support.

ĭn′ flù ĕn′ tial (-shal) — Exerting influence or power; having authority.

out rā′ ġeoŭs — Violent; furious; raging.

ĕm′ ĭ nent — High; lofty; distinguished; celebrated.

hōme′ stĕad — The home of a family; the place of origin.

ĭg′ nȯ rā′ mŭs — A stupid, ignorant person.

ĕp′ ĭ dĕm′ ĭe — Spreading widely; affecting great numbers.

ꞓŏn tā′ ġioŭs — Catching; conveying disease.

glō′ rĭ oŭs — Illustrious; famous; noble.

LESSON CCCXLII. Latin Roots.

cedo, cessum = *to yield;* **clino** = *to lean;* **flecto, flectum** = *to turn, bend.*

1. çĕde	7. çĕs' sion (sĕsh' ŭn)	13. ăe elĭv' I tў
2. çĕase	8. prò çĕs' sion	14. ĭn' elĭ nä' tion
3. ĕx çēed'	9. elĭn' Ie	15. rĕ flĕet'
4. rĕ çĕss'	10. dĕ eline'	16. flĕx' I ble
5. săe çēed'	11. rĕ elĭn' ĭng	17. çĭr' eŭm flĕx
6. prĕ çēde'	12. dĕ elĭv' I tў	18. dĕ flĕet'

19. ĭn flĕe' tion   20. rĕ flĕe' tor (-tĕr)

LESSON CCCXLIII. Latin Roots.

migro, migratum = *to remove;* **pello, pulsum** = *to drive;* **plico, plicatum** = *to fold.*

1. mĭ' grāte	7. pŭlse	13. ăp plў'
2. ĕm' I grant	8. dĭs pĕl'	14. eŏm' plĕx
3. mĭ' grà tò rў	9. ĭm' pŭlse	15. dĭs plaў'
4. trăns' mĭ grāte	10. ĕx pŭl' sion	16. sĭm' ple
5. ĭm mĭ grā' tion	11. pŭl sä' tion	17. plĭ' ant
6. rĕ pŭl' sion	12. dû plĭç' I tў	18. ĭm plĭç' ĭt

19. mŭl tĭ plĭç' I tў   20. ăe eŏm' plĭçe

LESSON CCCXLIV. Latin Roots.

pono, positum = *to place;* **porto, portatum** = *to carry;* **prehendo, prehensum** = *to take hold of.*

1. pŏst	7. ŏp pō' nent	13. ĭm' pŏr tū' nI tў
2. pŏs' tûre	8. ĭm' pŏrt	14. sûr prĭse'
3. prò pōse'	9. pŏr' tĕr	15. ăp' prĕ hĕnd'
4. pûr' pose	10. pŏrt' à ble	16. ĭm prĭs' on
5. rĕ pōse'	11. rĕ pŏrt' ĕr	17. eŏm prĕ hĕnd'
6. ŏp' pò sĭte	12. pŏrt fōl' iò (-yò)	18. ĕn' tĕr prĭse

19. ăp prĕn' tĭçe   20. eŏm prĕ hĕn' sion

LESSON CCCXLV. Synonyms.

These words are to be distinguished carefully from one another.

solicit
entreat
beseech
implore
supplicate

To *solicit* is to ask earnestly of one whom we address as a superior; to *entreat* implies a request enforced by reasons and arguments; to *beseech* is stronger than *entreat*, and is used more in poetry; to *implore* is resorted to by a sufferer for the relief of his misery, and is addressed to those who can avert or increase the calamity; to *supplicate* expresses the extreme of entreaty, and usually implies a state of deep humiliation. We *solicit* a favor; we *entreat* a judge to listen to our explanations; we *beseech* Heaven to hear our prayer; we *implore* the king to be merciful. we *supplicate* the general to spare the lives of the rebels taken in battle.

strong
robust

Strong denotes great physical ability; a *strong* man can lift a great weight. *Robust* implies strongly-built, with great power of endurance. A *robust* man can bear heat and cold, and carry on his work in spite of every kind of hardship.

take
bring
carry

To *take* is simply to lay hold of; to *bring* is to convey from a distant to a nearer place; to *carry* is to convey by sustaining the thing carried, and generally implies motion from the speaker. For example: *Take* that basket, and *bring* me some eggs from the grocer; *carry* them carefully, so as not to break them.

work
task

Work is that which calls for an exertion of strength; it is more or less voluntary; as, the man was happy at his *work*, for it was to bring him rest and comfort in his old days. A *task* is *work* imposed by others; as, the *task* was a tedious one.

LESSON CCCXLVI.

The prefix *con* means *with*. That it may be easier to pro
nounce it is changed to *com, col, co, cog,* and *cor.*

eŏn nĕet'	eŏm bīne'	eô ērçe'
eŏn çŝal'·	eŏl lāte'	eô ĕ' val
eŏn sĭɤn'	eŏl lĕet'	eŏg' nātc
eŏn' elāve	eŏl' lô quy̆	eŏg nĭ' tion
eŏn' eāve	eŏl lū' ŝion	eŏr rŭpt'
eŏm prĕss'	eô' à lĕsçe'	eŏr' rê lâte'
eŏm mánd'	eô' ăd jū' tor (-tēr)	eŏr' rê spŏnd'

LESSON CCCXLVII.

The English *counter* and the Latin *contra* mean *against;*
the prefix *circum* signifies *around.*

eoun' tēr ăet	eŏn' trà ry̆	çĭr eŭm serībe'
eoun' tēr fei̇t	eŏn' trà vēne'	çĭr eŭm' fēr ençe
eoun' tēr mánd'	eŏn' trà dīet'	çĭr eŭm lô eū' tion

LESSON CCCXLVIII.

The prefix *de* means *down* or *from; dis* signifies *off, to dĕ-
prive of,* or *not;* it sometimes drops the *s* and at other times
changes that letter to *f.*

dê jĕet'	dĭs grāçe'	dĭs ĭn hĕr' ĭt
dê eŏet'	dĭs pērse'	dĭs ĭn elīned'
dê flêet'	dĭs gu̇ĭŝe'	dĭs sĭm' ĭ lar (-lēr)
dê eămp'	dĭs' eount	dĭs săt' ĭs fy̆
dê elīne'	dĭs chärġe'	dĭs eŏn tĭn' ûe
dê frau̇d'	dĭs eȯv' ēr	dĭs ĕn chȧnt' ĕd
dê bau̇ch'	dĭs ħŏn' or (-ēr)	dĭ grĕss'
dê nounçe'	dĭs loy' al	dĭ rĕe' tion
dê serībe'	dĭs ɔ̇ blĭġe'	dĭf' fĭ dent
dê bĭl' ĭ tāte	dĭs mount' ĕd	dĭ mĭn' ĭsh
dê lĭn' ê āte	dĭs eȯl' ôred	dĭ lăp' ĭ dāte

LESSON CCCXLIX. Words hard to spell and their meaning.

trȧçe′ȧ ble	That may be followed by some mark or sign.
mĭs′ sĭle	A weapon thrown by the hand or by a machine.
wĕap′ ȯn	Any instrument used in destroying, defeating, or injuring an enemy.
chänge′ȧ ble	Subject to change; inconstant.
dĕf′ ẽr ençe	Submission to the wishes or opinion of another; great respect; reverence.
ȯe′ ṳ lĭst	Ono skilled in treating diseases of the eye.
hȧn̯d′ kẽr chĭef	A piece of cloth carried for wiping the face and hands.
hȯ′ sier (-zhẽr-) ў̆	Stockings in general.
shĕr′ ĭf ƒ	An officer of the law.
whirl′(hwẽrl′-)p͞ool	A current of water moving in a circular direction.
ĭm′ pĭ oŭs	Wanting in piety; irreligious.
prĭv′ ĭ lĕge	A right not enjoyed by others or by all.
vĭt′ rĭ ȯl	Sulphuric acid.
rĕt′ ĭ eūle	A little bag.
brĭg′ ȧ dĭẽr′	A military title.
pȧl′ ȧ tȧ ble	Agreeable to the taste.
vĕn′ ẽr ȧ ble	Deserving of honor and respect.
fȧb′ ṳ loŭs	Not real; exceeding great.
glŭt′ ton oŭs	Eating to excess.
prĕj′ ṳ dĭçe	An opinion or leaning unfavorable to anything, without just cause.
sȯe′ ṳ lar (-lẽr)	Relating to things not spiritual or holy.

LESSON CCCL. Latin Roots.

pendeo, pensum = *to hang ;* **rumpo, ruptum** = *to break ;*
scio, scitum = *to know.*

1. pĕnd' ent	7. pĕn' dù lŭm	13. eŏr rŭp' tion
2. sŭs pĕnse'	8. ăb rŭpt'	14. scī' ençe
3. ăp pĕn' dĭx	9. rŭp' tûre	15. eŏn'scious(-shŭs)
4. dĕ pĕnd'	10. ĭr rŭp' tion	16. eŏn'science(-shens)
5. dĕ pĕnd'ençe	11. bănk' rŭpt	17. scī ĕn tĭf' Ie
6. prŏ pĕn'sĭ tў	12. ĭn' tĕr rŭpt	18. prē'sci(-shī-)ençe

19. ŏm nĭs'cient(-nĭsh'ent)   20. ŏm nĭs'çiençe

LESSON CCCLI. Latin Roots.

scribo, scriptum = *to write ;* **sentio, sensum** = *to feel ;*
solvo, solutum = *to loose.*

1. serĭbe	7. sĕnse	13. dĭs sĕn' sion
2. serĭb' ble	8. sĕn' tençe	14. sŏlve
3. serĭp' tûre	9. sĕn' sĭ ble	15. sŏl' û ble
4. dĕ serĭp' tion	10. sĕn' su(-shu̧-)oŭs	16. ăb sŏlve'
5. prĕ serĭp'tion	11. sĕn' tĭ ment	17. sŏl' ven çў
6. măn' û serĭpt	12. sĕn' sĭ tĭve	18. ăb' sò lūte

19. ĭn sŏl' vent   20. rĕv' ò lū' tion

LESSON CCCLII. Latin Roots.

servo, servatum = *to save, to keep ;* **specio, spectum** = *to look ;*
spiro, spiratum = *to breathe.*

1. sērv' ant	7. sērv' ĭle	13. sŭs pĕet'
2. ŏb ṣĕrve'	8. spĕe' tēr	14. eŏn spĭe'û oŭs
3. prĕ ṣĕrve'	9. dĕ spĭṣe'	15. sprĭte
4. prĕ ṣĕrv' ēr	10. spē'cious	16. spĭr' ĭt
5. rĕṣ' ēr vā' tion	11. spĕç' Ĭ mĕn	17. ĭn spĭred'
6. ŏb ṣĕrv' à tò rў	12. spĕe' tà ele	18. spĭr' ĭt û al

19. ås pĭ rā' tion   20. eŏn spĭr' à çў

LESSON CCCLIII.

The Latin prefix *ex* means *out of, from* and *out;* it becomes *e, ec,* and *ef* for the sake of ease in pronunciation.

ĕx pĕl'	ĕx ‑elāim'	ê jĕet'	ĕe' stȧ sў
ĕx ẖôrt'	ĕx trȧet'	ê vȧde'	ĕe çĕn' trĭe
ĕx çĭte'	ĕx' ê erāte	ê rāse'	ĕf fūse'
ĕx pōrt'	ĕx' eȧ vāte	ê vŏlve'	ĕf fȧçe'
ĕx pănd'	ĕx' ŏr çĭẹe	ê mērġe'	ĕf' fēr vĕsce'
ĕx ‑elūde'	ĕx ‑erụ' çĭ âte	ê ‑elĭpse'	ĕf fĕm' ĭ nâte

LESSON CCCLIV.

The Greek prefix *epi* means *on, near, during;* the Latin prefix *extra* signifies *beyond.*

ĕp' ĭ grăm	ĕp' ĭ dērm' ĭs	ĕx trȧ' nê oŭs
ĕp' ĭ lŏgue	ĕp' ĭ glŏt' tĭs	ĕx' trȧ mū' ral
ĕp' ĭ dĕm' ĭe	ĕx' trȧ dĭ' tion	ĕx' trȧ ġē' nê oŭs
ĕp' ĭ lĕp' sў	ĕx trăv' ȧ gant	ĕx traôr' dĭ nȧ rў

LESSON CCCLV.

For, un, or *with* as a prefix to verbs have usually the force of negatives, denoting *against,* or *away, aside.*

fŏr bĭd'	fŏr sāke'	ŭn nērve'	ŭn lēarn' ĕd
fŏr gĕt'	fŏr sweâr'	ŭn ‑elȧsp'	wĭth hŏld'
fŏr gĭve'	ŭn fûrl'	ŭn stĕad' ў	wĭth drạw'
fŏr beâr'	ŭn vẹil'	ŭn hĕalth' ў	wĭth stănd'

LESSON CCCLVI.

The Latin *semi* and the Greek *hemi* mean *half.*

sĕm' ĭ tŏne	sĕm' ĭ quā' vēr	hĕm' ĭ trŏpe
sĕm' ĭ cō' lŏn	sĕm' ĭ lĭq' uĭd	hĕm' ĭ stĭeẖ
ᴈĕm' ĭ çĭr' ele	sĕm' ĭ ăn' nŭ al	hĕm' ĭ sphĕre

LESSON CCCLVII. Synonyms.

These words are to be distinguished carefully from one another.

temporary
transient
transitory
fleeting

Temporary is that which lasts only for a time; *transient*, that which is short at best; *transitory*, that which is liable soon to pass away; *fleeting*, that which is in the act of taking its flight. This world is only our *temporary* home; life is *transient*, its joys are *transitory*, its hours are *fleeting*.

temper
humor

Temper always shows itself to be the same whenever it shows itself at all; *humor* varies perpetually. Thus, we may be in the *humor* for reading or for writing, for what is lively or what is serious; but our *temper* is shown in our daily conduct.

tautology
repetition

Tautology is a *repetition* of the same meaning in different words. For example: *Down* until this time; hitherto and *before now*.

talk
conversation

Talk is usually broken, familiar, and variable; *conversation* is more continuous and sustained, and turns ordinarily upon topics of higher interest. Children *talk* to their parents or to their companions; men *converse* together.

trivial
trifling

Both these words are used to characterize objects of little importance or value. *Trivial*, however, generally implies contempt, while *trifling* does not. Thus, we say, "That is a *trivial* matter, hardly worth consideration;" "Our time was spent in amusements and other *trifling* matters."

tease
vex

Tease implies a prolonged annoyance in respect to little things, which is often more irritating and harder to bear than severe pain. *Vex* denotes the disturbance or anger created by minor provocations, etc. We are *teased* by the buzzing of a fly in our ears; we are *vexed* by the stupidity of a servant.

LESSON CCCLVIII. Homonyms.

rĭng, a circle.

wrĭng, to turn and strain with violence.

rāiṣed, caused to rise.

rāzed, leveled; overthrew.

rĭght, correct; just.

wrĭte, to form letters, figures, or characters.

rīte, form; ceremony.

wrĭght, a workman.

rōte, mere repetition, without attention to the meaning.

wrōte, did write.

rōe, a female deer.

rōw, persons or things arranged in a line.

rĕd, of the color of blood.

rĕad, did read.

rēed, a plant.

rēad, to go over and utter aloud, or recite to one's self.

rāiṣe, to cause to rise; to lift up.

rāyṣ, a number of lines coming out from one center.

rāze, to overthrow; to destroy.

LESSON CCCLIX. Dictation Exercise.

The rays of the setting sun look red. I have read of houses being razed to the ground by wind; it must blow hard to raze a house. I raised the dumb-bell to my shoulder, but could not raise it higher. My brother wrote to me last week, and it is only right that I should write to him. My little sister learned the lesson by rote from hearing me read it. I dropped my ring on the ground. Bam-boo is a reed. Five soldiers are standing in a row. There is a pretty roe in the Park. My brother is a wheelwright. If we, wring clothes too much in washing we may tear them. A rite is not a sacra-ment but only a form.

LESSON CCCLX. Latin Roots.

sto, statum = *to stand, to set;* **stringo, strictum** = *to bind;*
struo, structum = *to build.*

1. stā' ble	7. stāte	13. strĭn' ġent
2. stā' tion	8. strĭet	14. eŏn strāint'
3. dĭs' tant	9. strāin	15. dê stroy'
4. eŏn' stant	10. dĭs' trĭet	16. ĭn strŭet'
5. stā' tion â rў	11. dĭs trĕss'	17. strŭe' tûre
6. stănd' ard (-ērd)	12. rê strĭet'	18. eŏn' strue

19. ĭn' stru ment   20. ŏb strŭe' tion

LESSON CCCLXI. Latin Roots.

tango, tactum = *to touch;* **tendo, tensum** = *to stretch;*
teneo, tentum = *to hold, to keep.*

1. eŏn' tăet	7. eŏn tĭn' ġent	13. tĕnd' en çў
2. tăn' ġent	8. ĭn tĕnse'	14. ăt tĕnd' ançe
3. tăn' ġĭ ble	9. ăt tĕnd'	15. tĕn' ĕt
4. ĭn tăet'	10. prê tĕnçe'	16. tĕn' ant
5. ăt tăch'	11. ĕx tĕn' sion	17. eŏn tāin'
6. eŏn tā' ġiȯn	12. ĭn tĕn' tion	18. dê tĕn' tion

19. ăb' stĭ nençe   20. māin' tê nançe

LESSON CCCLXII. Latin Roots.

traho, tractum = *to draw;* **venio, ventum** = *to come;*
verbum = *word.*

1. trāçe	7. dĭs trăe' tion	13. prê vĕnt' ĭve
2. ăt trăet'	8. ăd' vĕnt	14. ăd vĕn' tûre
3. ĕx trăet'	9. eŏn vēne'	15. vērb
4. pōr trāy'	10. vĕn' tûre	16. prŏv' ērb
5. eŏn' trăet	11. ĭn vĕnt' or (-ēr)	17. vēr' bōse
6. ĕx trăe' tion	12. eȯv' ê nant	18. vēr' bĭ âġe

19. prô vēr' bĭ al   20. rᴬ vēr' bēr âte

LESSON CCCLXIII.

Words frequently mispronounced or improperly accented.

sch*ĭ*şm	sûr tǫut'	rĕd' ô lent
nĕth' ēr	mĭn' å rĕt	tăp' ĕs trў̆
ŏ' å sĭs	stạl' wart (-wērt)	plăt' ĭ nŭm
pā' thŏs	trăv' ērse	vĕr bā' tĭm
tĭ ā' rå	vĭr' ụ lent	å mĕ' nå ble
vĕn dūe'	ĭn hēr' *e*nt	trụ' eû lent
păġ' eant	hê răl' dĭe	vĭ' ô là ble
prŏv' ŏst	plê bē' ian (-y*a*n)	ăp' på rā' tŭs
sue çiṇet'	trĭ (trĭs-) sў̆l' là ble	vĭ tū' pēr āte

LESSON CCCLXIV. Words accented on the first syllable.

eòm' pass	eū' eŭm bēr	eŏṇ' grụ ent	eŏn' stĭ tūte
eŏn' dŭet	eăr' rĭa*g*e	ē' quĭ poişe	drăm' å tĭst
dū' rĕss	eŏn' strụe	ĕx' plê tô rў̆	erĭn' ô lĭne
grŏv' el	eŏs' tūme	dĭs' çĭ plĭne	bĕl' lows (-lŭs)
ê' pået	ĕq' uĭ tў̆	dròm' ê då rў̆	ăm' bēr grĭs

LESSON CCCLXV. Words accented on the second syllable.

dê fūṇet'	ĭm mŏ' bĭle	dĭs eòm' fĭt	ạu tŏm' å tŏn
gāin sāy'	ăs sĭ*g*n' ôr	åd ŭm' brāte	ảe eū' mù lāte
eû rā' tòr	dê eŏ' roùs	dĭ grĕs' sion	ăn nĭ' hĭ lāte
dĭş ăs' tēr	dĭ mĕn' sion	ål lŏp' å thў̆	är bĭt' rå ment

LESSON CCCLXVI. Words hard to spell and to pronounce.

e*h*ā' ŏs	ŏx' ĭde	gu*i*n' êa	g*h*ăst' lў̆
fạu' çĕt	dê' pŏ*t*	môr' tĭse	eû rê' kå
fē' tĭçh	eăr' tĕl	tôr' toĭse	ġuēr' dòn
vĕn' ûe	sĭb' ў̆l	nū*i*' sançe	frăn' chĭşe
moĭ' ê tў̆	mê' grĭm	r*h*ụ' bärb	mēer' scha*u*m
å bў̆ş' mal	g*h*ēr' kĭn	*ps*ў̆' e*h*l*e*	hĕm' ŏr r*h*ăg*.

LESSON CCCLXIX. Synonyms.

These words are to be distinguished carefully from one another.

vanity
pride

Vanity is the love of being admired (not merely approved), so that he who is vain has a secret feeling of pleasure at being praised for excellence which he commonly does not possess, and knows he does not possess. *Pride* is an over-valuing of one's self for some real or imagined superiority. A man may be *proud* of his acquirements, rank, talents, etc.; he is *vain* of his personal appearance, his fine clothes, etc.

valuable
precious
costly

Valuable signifies having worth; *precious* having a high price; *costly*, costing much money. A book is often *valuable* for its contents; a thankful heart is like a box of *precious* ointment; there are many *costly* things which are *valuable* to those only who spend their money for them.

vagabond
vagrant
tramp
beggar

Vagabond, vagrant, and *tramp* have all about the same meaning, and stand for a strolling, idle, worthless fellow having no fixed dwelling; a *beggar* is simply one who asks for alms. A *vagabond, vagrant,* or *tramp* may not be a *beggar;* a *beggar* need not necessarily be a *vagabond, vagrant,* or *tramp.*

voluntary
spontaneous

What is *voluntary* is an act of choice; what is *spontaneous* springs wholly from feeling by a kind of outburst of the mind which admits of no reflection; as a *spontaneous* burst of applause. Hence the term is sometimes applied to things inanimate; abstinence is *voluntary* fasting, and exercise but *voluntary* labor.

want
wish

We *want* that which we need; we *wish* for that which will add to our comfort or pleasure: We *want* bread; we *wish* for a fortune.

LESSON CCCLXX. Words often Confounded.

dĕ' çent, suitable; proper.

dĕ scĕnt', extraction; attack; slope.

dĭs sĕnt', difference of opinion.

dĕf' ēr ençe, respect.

dĭf'fēr ençe, dissimilarity.

dạwn, break of day.

dŏn, to put on.

dōse, the quantity of medicine to be taken at one time.

dōze, to sleep lightly.

de çẹased', dead.

dĭş ẹaşed', afflicted with a sickness.

dĕ vīçe', a contrivance; an invention.

dĕ vīşe', to plan.

dĕp rả vä' tion, the state of being corrupt or wicked.

dẹp'rĭ vä' tion, loss; want.

drŏss, waste matter.

drạwş, pulls along.

ĕs sä𝑦', to attempt.

ăs sä𝑦', to subject to a chemical examination.

LESSON CCCLXXI. Dictation Exercise.

The boy draws the cart as well as a man would. Out of deference to the family of the deceased we should devise some means to give him decent burial; The doctor gave the patient a dose to relieve a diseased lung. I suffer from deprivation of sleep, for I only doze occasionally. If we essay to assay the metal we should devise some device to save the dross. Although there may be some difference of opinion in our club, no voice is raised in dissent. We started at dawn to go up the mountain, first stopping to don our heavy clothing. My father can trace his descent back two hundred years. The prisoner's crime showed unusual depravation.

LESSON CCCLXXII. Latin Roots.

sumo, sumptum = *to take;* **salio, saltum** = *to jump;*
sacer = *sacred.*

1. ăs sūme′
2. rê ṣūme′
3. prê ṣūme′
4. sŭmp′ tû oŭs
5. rê ṣŭmp′ tion
6. ăs sŭmp′ tion

7. eŏn sūme′
8. săl′ lў
9. ĭn′ sŭlt
10. rê ṣŭlt′
11. ăs saẓlt′
12. ăs săĭl′

13. sā′ lĭ ent
14. ĕx aẓl tā′ tion
15. săe′rĭ fīce(-fīz)
16. săe′ rĭ lĕge
17. săe′ ră ment
18. eŏn′ sê erāte

19. dĕs′ ê erāte   20. ĕx′ ê erȧ ble

LESSON CCCLXXIII. Latin Roots.

veho, vectum = *to carry;* **verto, versum** = *to turn;* **verus** = *true.*

1. eŏn vęẏ′
2. eŏn′ vĕx
3. ĭn vęigh′
4. vĕ′ hĭ ele
5. vĕx ā′ tion
6. vê′ hê ment

7. ĭn vêe′ tĭve
8. vērse
9. vēr′ sion
10. ăd vērt′
11. ȧ vēr′ sion
12. ăd vēr′ sĭ tў

13. vēr′ sȧ tĭle
14. ăd′ vēr tĭṣe′
15. ȧ vēr′
16. vēr′ dĭet
17. vēr′ ĭ fў
18. vê rā′cious

19. vê răç′ ĭ tў   20. vēr′ ĭ tȧ ble

LESSON CCCLXXIV. Latin Roots.

via = *way;* **unus** = *one;* **sequor, secutus** = *to follow.*

1. dê′ vĭ āte
2. trĭv′ ĭ al
3. dê′ vĭ oŭs
4. prê′ vĭ oŭs
5. ŏb′ vĭ oŭs
6. ĭm pēr′ vĭ oŭs

7. ŏb′ vĭ āte
8. ū′ nĭt
9. û nīte′
10. û′ nĭ tў
11. û′ nĭ fôrm
12. ūn′ ion(-yŭn)

13. û nīque′(-nēk′)
14. û′ nĭ eŏrn
15. sê′ quĕl
16. sê′ quĕnçe
17. ĕx′ ê eūte
18. sŭb′sê quent

19. eŏn sêe′ û tĭve   20. pēr′ sê eū′ tioᴌ

LESSON CCCLXXV.

The prefix *per* means *through;* *pre* signifies *before;* *pan* is
the Greek word for *all;* and *poly* the Greek for *many.*

pĕr sĭst' ent	prê çĕd' ençe	păn' thê ĭşm
pēr' eô lāte	prê şŭmp' tion	păn' tô mīme
pēr' pê trāte	prĕj' û dĭçe	păn' tô grȧph
pēr ăm' bû lāte	prê sĕn' tĭ ment	păn' ȧ çê' ȧ
prê vĕn' tion	prê vȧr' ĭ eāte	păn' ô rä' mȧ
prê eûr' sor	prĕp' ȧ rā' tion	pŏl' ў glŏt
prē' mȧ tūre'	prê dŏm' ĭ nāte	pŏl' ў thê' ĭşm

LESSON CCCLXXVI.

The prefix *re* means *again, back; retro, backwards; sub,*
under or *below,* the *b* in the last word is sometimes changed
to *c, f, g, p, r, s,* and *m.*

rê view'	rê' trô grāde	sŭg ġĕst'
rê dēem'	rê' trô grĕs' sion	sŭp prĕss'
rê scĭnd'	sŭb mĭt'	sŭp plănt'
rê' ĭm bûrse'	sŭb serībe'	sûr pàss'
rê vēr' bēr ȧte	sŭb mērġe'	sûr mount'
rê ġĕn' ēr ȧte	sŭb ôr' dĭ nȧte	sŭs pĕnd'
rê sŭs' çĭ tāte	sŭe çĭṇet'	sŭs tāin'
rê' trô spêet	sŭf fûşe'	sŭm' mȯn

LESSON CCCLXXVII.

The prefix *super* means *above; se, apart; syn* (written also
sym and *syl*), *together.*

sū' pēr sēde'	sū' pēr ĭn dūçe'	sўm' pȧ thў
sū' pēr vēne'	sē dĭ' tion	sўm' bŏl ĭze
sû pēr' lȧ tĭve	sĕg' rē gȧte	sўmp' tȯm
sû pēr' flû oŭs	sē çĕs' sion	sўl' lȧ ble
sū' pēr çĭl' ĭ oŭs	sўn' thê sĭs	sўl' lȧ bŭs

LESSON CCCLXXVIII. Synonyms.

These words are to be distinguished carefully from one another.

safety
security

Safety implies the absence of danger; *security* the absence of all fear of danger. *Safe* refers to the present; *secure* to the future. Those who are out of danger are *safe;* those who are beyond the reach or the fear of danger are *secure.* Thus, we say, complete *safety;* well-grounded or false *security.*

scholar
pupil

A *scholar* is one who is, or has been, under instruction; a *pupil* is one under the immediate and personal care of a teacher. The term *scholar* is applied to both young and old; *pupil* only to the young. Thus, we say, a distinguished *scholar;* an obedient *pupil.*

singular
remarkable

That which is unusual, out of the ordinary course of things, is *singular;* that which is worthy of being noticed is *remarkable.* Thus, it is *singular* that during the whole time I was away traveling I saw very little, if anything that was *remarkable.*

surpass
excel

We may *surpass* without any direct effort; we cannot *excel* without effort. Thus, one man by his genius may *surpass* another, but no one can *excel* in any art except by study and application. Thus, we say, though the boy can not hope to surpass his brother, as a rule he *excels* him in mathematics.

specimen
sample

A *specimen* is a representation of the class of things to which it belongs; as, my cabinet contains *specimens* of every mineral found in the state. A *sample* is a part of the thing itself used as a fair representation of the whole; as, a *sample* of sugar, a *sample* of cloth; a commercial traveler carries *samples* of the goods he is trying to sell.

LESSON CCCLXXIX. Words often confounded.

căp′ ĭ tal, principal, chief city.

căp′ ĭ tŏl, the house occupied by the United States Congress.

cŏn dĕmn′, to blame.

cŏn tĕmn′, to despise.

cŭr′ rant, a fruit.

cŭr′rent, a stream; course.

căn, to be able.

kĕn, reach of sight or knowledge.

crĭck, a pain in some part of the body making it difficult to move the part affected.

crēek, a small river or brook.

chŏ′ ral, sung in chorus.

cŏr′ al, a limy deposit made by certain animals, and used as an ornament.

cŏm′ ĭ tỹ, civility; good breeding.

cŏm mĭt′ tĕe, one or more persons to whom any matter or business is referred.

çĕn′ sŭs, an official numbering of inhabitants.

sĕns′ ĕṣ, feelings.

LESSON CCCLXXX. Dictation Exercise.

The Capitol stands in Washington, the capital of the United States. Much as we may contemn the fault, let us not condemn the man. The choral portions were very well sung, and charmed our senses. Whilst pulling against the current I got a crick in my back. The water in the creek is very low. There is a black currant bush in our garden. My sister has a coral necklace. I can read almost any writing, but a letter received to-day is beyond my ken. The committee has just finished the census; its proceedings were marked by great comity.

LESSON CCCLXXXI. Latin Roots.

tribuo, tribitum = *to give;* **video, visum** = *to see;* **omnis** = *all.*

1. trĭb′ ûte
2. trĭb′ û tå rў
3. ăt′ trĭ bûte
4. eŏn trĭb′ ûte
5. dĭs trĭb′ ûte
6. rĕt′rĭ bû′tion

7. rė̇ trĭb′ û tĭve
8. dĭs′trĭ bū′tion
9. vĭş′ åģe
10. vĭş′ ĭ ble
11. rė̇ vĭşe′
12. vĭş′ ĭt or(-ĕr)

13. vĭ′sion(vĭzh′ŭn)
14. ĕv′ ĭ dençe
15. prŏv′ ĭ dençe
16. ŏm′ nĭ bŭs
17. ŏm nĭp′ ô tent
18. ŏm nĭv′ ô roŭs

19. ŏm nĭp′ ô tençe   20. ŏm nĭs′ cient(nĭsh′ ent)

LESSON CCCLXXXII. Latin Roots.

vivo, victum = *to live;* **voco, vocatum** = *to call;* **primus** = *first.*

1. vĭv′ ĭd
2. rė̇ vĭve′
3. vĭv′ ĭ fў
4. sûr vĭve′
5. rė̇ vĭv′ al
6. vĭ vā′cious(-shŭs)

7. eŏn vĭv′ ĭ al
8. voiçe
9. vŏ′ eal
10. vow′ ĕl
11. rė̇ vŏke′
12. eŏn vŏke′

13. vouch′ ĕr
14. vŏ′ eal ĭst
15. ĭn′ vŏ eā′ tion
16. prĭme
17. prĭm′ ĕr
18. prĭ′ måte

19. prī′ må rў   20. prĭm′ ĭ tĭve

LESSON CCCLXXXIII. Latin Roots.

volvo, volutum = *to roll;* **seco, sectum** = *to cut;* **rego, rectum** = *to rule.*

1. rė̇ vōlt′
2. ė̇ vŏlve′
3. vŏl′ ûme
4. vŏl′ û ble
5. dė̇ vĕl′ ŏp
6. ĕv ô lū′ tion

7. rĕv′ ô lū′ tion
8. sĕet
9. ĭn′ sĕet
10. dĭs sĕet′
11. sĕe′ tion
12. sĕg′ ment

13. dĭs sĕe′ tion
14. ĭn′tĕr sĕe′ tion
15. rẹiģn
16. rĕe′ tor(-tĕr)
17. rē′ gal
18. rē′ ģent

19. dĭ rẹet′   20. rĕg′ ĭs tĕr

Abbreviations used in Writing and Printing.

For other abbreviations see pages 32, 47, 56, and 58.

@, at.

Adjt., Adjutant.

Æt. or **æt.** (*ætatis*), of age, aged.

Ag., Aggeus.

Alex., Alexander.

A. M. or **M. A.**(*artium magister*), Master of Arts.

A. M. D. G. (*Ad majorem Dei gloriam*), to the greater glory of God.

And., Andrew.

Anon., anonymous.

Anth., Anthony.

Ap., Apostle.

Arch., Archibald.

Agt., Agent.

ad lib. (*ad libitum*), at pleasure.

Atty., Attorney.

Atty.-Gen., Attorney-General.

Aug., Augustus.

Av. or **Ave.**, Avenue.

Avoir., avoirdupois.

Bart., Baronet.

B. C., before Christ.

Benj., Benjamin.

Brig.-Gen., Brigadier-General.

B. Sc., Bachelor of Science.

bu., bushels.

¢. or **ct.**, cents.

Cap., capital. **Caps.**, capitals.

Card., Cardinal.

Cath., Catholic.

C. E., civil engineer.

cf. (*confer*), compare.

Ch., Church.

Chas., Charles.

Chron., Chronicles.

Co., Company.

c/o, in care of.

C. O. D., Collect on delivery.

Col., Colossians.

Coll., College; Collector.

C. M., Vincentian Fathers.

C. P., Passionist Fathers.

C. PP. S., Congregation of the Most Precious Blood.

C. R., Fathers of the Resurrection.

Cr., credit; creditor.

C. S. B., Basilian Fathers.

C. S. C., Congregation of the Holy Cross.

C. S. P., Paulist Fathers.

C. S. Sp., Fathers of the Holy Ghost.

C. SS. R., Redemptorist Fathers.

d., days; pence.

Dan. or **Danl.**, Daniel.

D. C. L., Doctor of Civil Law.

D. D. S., Doctor of Dental Surgery.

Deut., Deuteronomy.

D. G. (*Dei gratia*), by the grace of God.

Dist.-Atty., District-Attorney.

Dr., debtor.

D. V. (*Deo volente*), God willing.
Dwt. or **dwt.**, pennyweight.
E., East.
ea., each.
Eccl., Ecclesiastes.
Ecclus., Ecclesiasticus.
Ed., edition.
Edm., Edmund.
Edw., Edward.
e. g. (*exempli gratia*), for example.
Eng., English; England.
Eph., Ephesians.
et al. (*et alibi*), and elsewhere.
et al. (*et alii*), and others.
et seq. (*et sequentia*), and following.
etc. or **&c.** (*et cætera*), and others; and so forth.
Ex., Example; Exodus.
Ezech., Ezechiel.
E. & O. E., errors and omissions excepted.
Fahr. or **F.**, Fahrenheit (thermometer).
Fr., French; France.
Fran., Francis.
Fred., Frederick.
Fri., Friday.
ft., feet.
Ft., Fort.
fur., furlong.
Gal., Galatians.
gal., gallons.
G. A. R., Grand Army of the Republic.
Gen., Genesis.
Geo., George.
gr., grains.
h., hours.
Hab., Habacuc.
H. B. M., His (or Her) Britannic Majesty.

hdkf., handkerchief.
Heb., Hebrews.
hhd., hogsheads.
H. M., His (or Her) Majesty.
H. R. H., His (or Her) Royal Highness.
ib. or **ibid.** (*ibidem*), in the same place.
id. (*idem*), the same.
i. e. (*id est*), that is.
I. H. S. (*Jesus Hominum Salvator*), Jesus the Saviour of Men; an abbreviation of *IHΣOYΣ*, the Greek form of the word *Jesus*.
in., inches.
incog. (*incognito*), unknown.
I. N. R. I. (*Iesus Nazarenus, Rex Iudæorum*), Jesus of Nazareth, King of the Jews.
in trans. (*in transitu*), on the passage.
inst., instant; the present month.
Isa., Isaias.
Jas., James.
Jer., Jeremias.
J. F., St. Joseph's Society of the Sacred Heart.
J. M. J., Jesus, Mary, Joseph.
Jona., Jonathan.
Jos., Joseph.
Jos., Josue.
J. P., Justice of the Peace.
Jr. or **jun.**, junior.
Judg., Judges.
l., line; **ll.**, lines.
l. or **£**, pounds sterling.
Lam., Lamentations.
L., Latin.
lb. or **℔** (*libra* or *libræ*), pound or pounds in weight.

l. c., lower case (small letter).

Lev., Leviticus.

L. I., Long Island.

Lieut., Lieutenant.

LL. B. (*Legum Bacclaaureus*), Bachelor of Laws.

LL. D. (*Legum Doctor*), Doctor of Laws.

L. S. (*locus sigilli*), place of the seal.

M. or **Mons.,** Monsieur.

M. (*meridies*), noon.

m., miles; minutes.

Mad. or **Mme.,** Madam.

Maj., Major.

Mal., Malachias.

Matth., Matthew.

M. C., Member of Congress.

M. D. (*Medicinæ Doctor*), Doctor of Medicine.

Mdlle., Mademoiselle.

mdse., merchandise.

Mem., memorandum; memoranda.

Messrs., Gentlemen.

Mich., Micheas.

Mgr., Monsignor.

Mlle , Mademoiselle.

mo., month; **mos.,** months.

Mon., Monday.

M. P., Member of Parliament.

Mr., Mister.

Mrs., Mistress (pron. Missis).

MS., manuscript.

M. S., Missionaries of La Salette.

M. S. C., Missionaries of the Sacred Heart.

MSS., manuscripts.

Mt., Mountain.

N., North.

N. A., North America.

Nath., Nathaniel.

N. B. (*nota bene*), mark well.

N. E., New England.

N. O., New Orleans.

No. (*numero*), number.

N. S. T. C. (*Noster Salvator Jesus Christus*), Our Saviour Jesus Christ.

Ob. or **ob.** (*obiit*), died.

O. C., Order of Charity.

O. C. C., Carmelites.

O. M. C., Minor Conventuals of St. Francis.

O. M. Cap., Capuchins.

O. M. I., Oblates of Mary Immaculate.

O. P., Dominicans.

O. S., Servites.

O. S. A., Augustinians.

O. S. B., Benedictines.

O. S. F., Franciscans.

O. S. H., Oblates of Sacred Heart.

Oxon. (*Oxonia*), Oxford.

oz., ounces.

p., page; **pp.,** pages.

Payt. or **payt.,** payment.

per cent. or **per ct.** (*per centum*) or %, by the hundred.

Ph. D. (*Philosophiæ Doctor*), Doctor of Philosophy.

Phil., Philip; Philippians.

Phila., Philadelphia.

pk., pecks.

P. M., Postmaster.

P. M. or **p. m.** (*post meridiem*), afternoon.

P. O., post-office.

P. P., parish priest.

P. P. C. (*pour prendre congé*), to take leave.

Pres., President.

Prof., Professor.

pro tem. (*pro tempore*), for the time being.

Prov., Proverbs.

prox. (*proximo*), the next month.

P. S., postscript.

Ps., Psalms.

P. S. M., Pious Society of Missions.

pt., pint or pints.

P. T. O., please turn over.

pwt., pennyweights.

qt., quart or quarts.

q. v. (*quod vide*), which see.

Qy., query.

rd., rod or rods.

Recd., received.

Rev., Reverend; Revelation.

Robt., Robert.

Rom., Romans (Book of); Roman letters.

R. R., Railroad.

R. S. V. P. (*repondez s'il vous plait*), answer if you please.

Rt. Hon., Right Honorable.

Rt. Rev., Right Reverend.

S., South.

s., shillings.

S. A., South America.

Saml. or **Sam.**, Samuel.

Sat., Saturday.

Sec., Secretary.

sec., seconds.

S. J., Jesuits.

S. M., Marists.

S. P. M., Fathers of Mercy.

sq. ft., square feet.

sq. in., square inches.

sq. m., square miles.

St., Street; Saint.

S. T. D. (*Sacræ Theologiæ Doctor*), Doctor of Divinity.

Sun., Sunday.

Supt., Superintendent.

T., tons; tuns.

T. A. B., Total Abstinence Brotherhood.

Theo., Theodore.

Theoph., Theophilus.

Thess., Thessalonians.

Thos., Thomas.

Thurs., Thursday.

Tim., Timothy.

tr., transpose.

Treas., Treasurer.

Tues., Tuesday.

ult. (*ultimo*), last, last month.

U. S. or **U. S. A.**, United States of America; United States Army.

U. S. M., United States Mail.

U. S. N., United States Navy.

V. A., Vicar Apostolic.

Ven., Venerable.

V. G., Vicar-General.

v. g. (*verbi gratia*), for example.

V. Rev., Very Reverend.

Vice-Pres., Vice-President.

viz. (*videlicet*), to wit, namely.

vol., volume.

vs. (*versus*), against.

W., West.

Wed., Wednesday.

wk., weeks.

Wm., William.

Wt., weight.

Xmas, Christmas.

Xt., Christ.

yd., yard or yards.

y. or **yr.**, year or years.

yrs., yours.

Zach., Zacharias.

& Co., and Company.

Spa ghet'ti

Can you spell spa-ghet-ti?

That is a hard word, but it is easy to eat.

You do not have to spell it.

You will like it the way Heinz makes it.

Ask your mother when you go home to have Heinz Spa-ghet-ti for dinner.

Tell her it will make her no trouble, as it is already cooked.

She will only have to heat it.

And you will have the joy of eating it.

Bab and Betty, Lou and Letty
Insist on having Heinz Spaghetti,
But Bill and Bobby, Tom and Tony
All prefer Heinz Macaroni.

H. J. HEINZ COMPANY *57 Varieties*

THE KING AND QUEEN MIGHT EAT THEREOF
AND NOBLEMEN BESIDES

WHEN Good Arthur ruled this land,
He was a goodly king,
He took three bags of barley meal
To make a bag pudding.

WHEN that good king his pudding made,
No doubt he worked for hours
A-mixing spices, fruit, and nuts,
And many kinds of flours.

And when that bag pudding was done
And all his courtiers ate,
We are not told what pains ensued
To him who cleared his plate.

Though you be neither king nor queen,
Yet you can make a dish
More luscious than their bag pudding
And fine as kings might wish.

From six fruit JELL-O's you may choose
A flavor sharp or mild,
And there you have a dessert rare
That's good for man and child.

YOURS FOR THE ASKING

There are six pure fruit flavors of JELL-O: Strawberry, Raspberry, Lemon, Orange, Cherry, Chocolate. The new JELL-O Book, just out, is more beautiful and complete than any other issued. It will be sent free, but be sure your name and address are plainly written.

"America's Most Famous Dessert"

JELL-O
THE GENESEE PURE
FOOD COMPANY
Le Roy, N.Y. Bridgeburg, Ont.

Reprinted by permission of John Martin's Book, The Child's Magazine.

"Oh, Billy, Don't You Just Love Postum?"

Growing boys and girls should not drink coffee or tea. But they *can* always enjoy a nice hot cup of Postum at breakfast or supper, without fear of harm.

No other mealtime drink is quite so healthful and appetizing in the morning before you start for school, because Postum is pure, wholesome and delicious.

Postum is made from choice wheat—the king of all the grains.

Mother will be glad to give you Postum every day, if you ask her.

Postum *for* HEALTH

"There's a Reason"

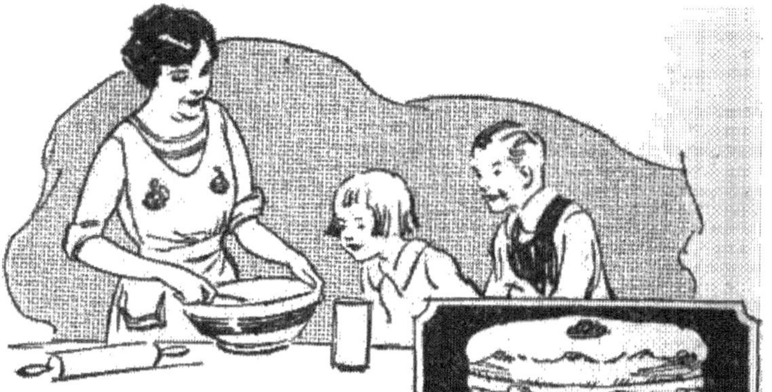

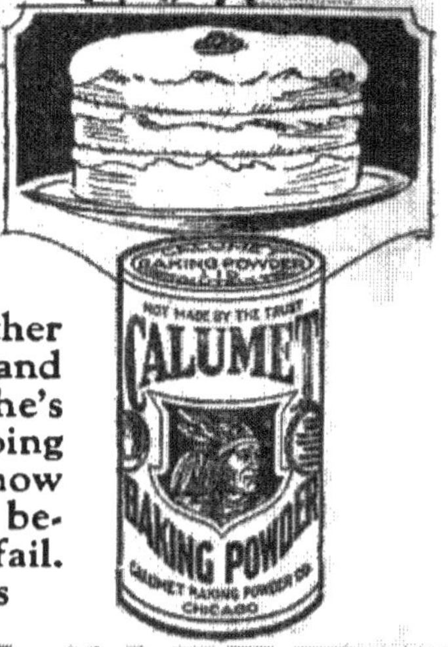

Waiting to Lick the Bowl

One half is mine and the other is brother's. And we just stand and watch mother when she's baking and wonder who's going to have the most. And we know the cake is going to be good because mother's cakes never fail. She says it's because she uses

CALUMET

The Economy Baking Powder

So when she sends us to the store for a can of it you just bet we run lickety-split, because we know then we are going to have a lot of goodies to eat.

Mother says she doesn't know how she could bake without us. But we know better. It's the little fellow we bring home from the store — the Calumet Kid, that she couldn't get along without when she wants to bake.

Millions of mothers are relying on Calumet — depending on it to produce pure, sweet and wholesome bakings every time they bake — and no one is ever disappointed.

Boys and girls—send your name and address for the FREE Calumet Puzzle.

CALUMET BAKING POWDER CO.
4100 Fillmore Street **Chicago, Illinois**

THE WORLD'S GREATEST BAKING POWDER

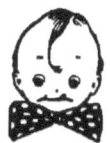

117 Popular Catholic Books for Everybody at 85c.

Each volume, attractively bound, net, 85c. Postage 10 cents.

ALTHEA. Nirdlinger.
BETWEEN FRIENDS. Aumerle.
BROWNIE AND I. Aumerle.
CHILDREN OF THE LOG CABIN. Delamare.
CLARE LORAINE. Lee.
DEAR FRIENDS. Nirdlinger.
FIVE BIRDS IN A NEST. Delamare.
FREDDY CARR'S ADVENTURES. Garrold, S.J.
FREDDY CARR AND HIS FRIENDS. Garrold, S.J.
HARMONY FLATS. Whitmire.
HOW THEY WORKED THEIR WAY. Egan.
IN QUEST OF THE GOLDEN CHEST. Barton.
JACK HILDRETH ON THE NILE. Taggart.
JUNIORS OF ST. BEDE'S, THE. Bryson.

KLONDIKE PICNIC, A. Donnelly.
LITTLE MARSHALLS AT THE LAKE, THE. Nixon-Roulet.
MILLY AVELING. Smith.
MYSTERY OF HORNBY HALL. Sadlier.
MYSTERY OF CLEVERLY. Barton.
NED RIEDER. Wehs.
NEW SCHOLAR AT ST. ANNE'S, THE. Brunowe.
PETRONILLA, AND OTHER STORIES. Donnelly.
POVERINA. Buckenham.
TALISMAN, THE. Sadlier.
TOLD IN THE TWILIGHT. Salome.
TREASURE OF NUGGET MOUNTAIN, THE. Taggart.
WINNETOU, THE APACHE KNIGHT. Taggart.
FIVE O'CLOCK STORIES. By a Religious.
LEGENDS AND STORIES OF THE HOLY CHILD JESUS FROM MANY LANDS. Lutz.
MORE FIVE O'CLOCK STORIES. By a Religious.
TALES AND LEGENDS OF THE MIDDLE AGES. Capella.

STANDARD 60 CENT JUVENILE LIBRARY

Each volume attractively bound, net, 60 cents. Postpaid, 65 cents.

ADVENTURE WITH THE APACHES, AN. Ferry.
AS TRUE AS GOLD. Mannix.
BELL FOUNDRY, THE. V. Schaching.
BERKLEYS, THE. Wight.
BISTOURI. Melandri.
BLISSYLVANIA POST-OFFICE, THE. Taggart.
BOB O'LINK. Waggaman.
RUNT AND BILL. Mulholland.
BY BRANSCOME RIVER. Taggart.
CHILDREN OF CUPA, THE. Mannix.
NAN NOBODY. Waggaman.
OLD CHARLMONT'S SEED-BED. Smith.

PANCHO AND PANCHITA. Mannix.
PAULINE ARCHER. Sadlier.
PERIL OF DIONYSIO, THE. Mannix.
PILGRIM FROM IRELAND, A. Carnot.
QUEEN'S PAGE, THE. Hinkson.
RECRUIT TOMMY COLLINS. Bonesteel.
SEA-GULL'S ROCK, THE. Sandeau.
SEVEN LITTLE MARSHALLS. Roulet.
SUMMER AT WOODVILLE, A. Sadlier.

Complete List of Juveniles Free on Application.

Our 100-page Catalogue Sent Free Upon Request